*

When the eighteen-year-old Victoria became Queen of England she was horrified to learn that for twenty-eight years her father, the Duke of Kent, had lived with a mistress.

Yet there was never anything shameful in the association, no scandal ever disrupted the love between the Duke and the beautiful, gay and witty Madame Julie de St Laurent.

So why then *did* he finally break with her? His plea was that duty came before love. And his duty was to marry and produce an heir for the English throne.

But in *Royal Mistress* their joint lives are traced, from the garrison Rock of Gibraltar to the icy wastes of Canada and finally to the ostentatious salons of Society in Georgian London. And a different conclusion is reached: that it was not duty but pride; one more vainglorious effort, after a lifetime's thwarted ambitions, to achieve popularity and the esteem of the country.

Rose Meadows

Royal Mistress

ARROW BOOKS

ARROW BOOKS LTD
3 Fitzroy Square, London W1

AN IMPRINT OF THE HUTCHINSON GROUP

London Melbourne Sydney Auckland
Wellington Johannesburg Cape Town
and agencies throughout the world

*

First published simultaneously by
Hurst & Blackett Ltd and
Arrow Books Ltd 1972

*Made and printed in Great Britain
by The Anchor Press Ltd,
Tiptree, Essex*
ISBN 0 09 905550 3

Acknowledgement

The typescript of this novel was already in the hands of my publisher when Mrs Mollie Gillen's biography *The Prince and his Lady* was published.

I was so convinced by Mrs Gillen's findings that, recognising truth as opposed to legend, I felt I must correct certain incidents so as to present the true facts to my readers.

I am therefore deeply indebted to Mrs Gillen and wish to tender my very grateful thanks to her for the use of certain information, hitherto unpublished.

Prologue

It was not the beauty of the early June morning that had tempted His Majesty King George III to walk across the gardens of Kew Palace.

There, on the farther side, his six eldest sons were the occupants of three adjoining houses, and this six o'clock o' the morning visit was part of a daily routine to instil into them the benefits of early rising, Papa himself knocking on each bedroom door.

This morning, one of the occupants, Prince Edward, was fully awake when the sharp rap-tap sounded, followed by his father's guttural query, 'Have you had a good night's sleep, my son?'

The answer came quickly. 'Thank you, Sir, yes. I have slept well, Papa.'

That was not strictly true, the boy ruminated as he listened to the footsteps move on to William's door, but to admit that he had slept badly would have meant a visit from the surgeon to bleed him. Mama was a firm believer that bleeding was a certain cure for all ills, be it a headache or a stomach ache; inability to sleep or inability to rouse with the dawn.

This morning he had awakened before it was light, watching the dawn slowly filter through the drapes, a sense of depression weighing down on him, a gnawing, nagging misery that precluded all further sleep.

Today, fourteen-year-old William, the brother who until now had shared this house with him, was entering the

Royal Navy. That meant he, Edward, would be living alone, save for his tutors and the servants. True, his brothers George, Prince of Wales and Frederick lived in the adjoining house, but they were so much older and had no time for a twelve-year-old. At times, William had consorted with them, returning with such lurid tales of their way of living, their valets smuggling young ladies of the town into the house, their tutors totally unaware of what was going on. Not that he wanted to join them. The bawdy tales that William so relished in repeating, sickened him. It was a pity that his brothers, six-year-old Augustus and eight-year-old Ernest, living on the other side were too young to be companionable. He could see nothing but loneliness stretching out ahead of him. Perhaps when he was fourteen, his father would allow him to enter the army or the navy, but two years was a terrible long time to wait.

His valet came into the room, drew back the drapes and poured cold water into the basin on the marble wash-stand, looking significantly at his young master, who was making no attempt to rise.

Edward was wrestling with his problem. Would it be any use trying to explain to his parents his feeling of desolation? Would they consider Augustus and Ernest joining him, young as they were? At least the sound of their voices and their running around would dispel the gloom. No, he decided; neither Mama nor Papa had any love for him. Mama only loved George and Frederick, while Papa doted on the girls and the little ones. Indeed, since he had broken that clock, Papa seemed to hate him. Perhaps his older brothers were right. He shouldn't have owned up.

Memories of the incident came flooding back. It was an old clock, hanging on the landing wall just outside his bedroom door; a clock that never kept correct time, sometimes losing; sometimes gaining; sometimes stopping even when fully wound, and on that particular night, when everyone was in bed, it suddenly began to chime. On and on it went, until he could stand it no longer. He only meant to give it a little shake, but almost as soon as he touched it, it crashed to the ground, a little door on the back flying open, disgorging a tangle of coils and little-teethed wheels. He was back in bed in a flash, trembling with fear as to what the outcome would be.

No-one came to him, and when, next morning, the King knocked on his door, there was still no mention of the matter, until walking across to the Palace for breakfast at eight, William remarked, 'Did you see the old clock on the floor? It must have fallen during the night.' He wanted to confide in his brother, but something held him back, and it wasn't until they had breakfasted on their customary milk and dry bread and were ready to go to the schoolroom that the King spoke.

'I was deeply grieved this morning, to discover that some miscreant had smashed one of the clocks in his establishment. Will the miserable sinner step forward.'

Edward hadn't hesitated, hoping against hope that he would be allowed to speak; hoping that someone else had heard that incessant striking.

'So . . . you. I might have known. Wicked boy! Wicked boy! Wicked boy!' Edward watched his father's face taking on a purple hue. 'Destructive boy! Despoiler! Mr. Magendie, thrash the boy! Let the others learn what they can expect when they destroy another's property.'

There and then, he had to bend over a chair, while Mr. Magendie had viciously wielded his cane. The humiliation was two-fold, in that his sisters were present, but if his father, mother or tutor expected him to cry out, they were disappointed. Though he could taste the blood in his mouth, caused by his teeth biting into his lips, no sound escaped him, and it was only when the sobbing of his sisters became louder and louder that the King ordered Mr. Magendie to cease.

There had been no sympathy from his brothers.

'In the name of God,' demanded George, 'why did you have to own up?'

'He would never have known, but what it fell from the wall. . . .'

'You deserve **what** you got, for being so damned truthful,' had been William's caustic comment. 'I'd have lied and lied until I was black in the face. . . .'

'Sir.' It was his valet. 'You will be late, if you do not wash and dress now.'

Slowly, Edward slid out of bed. There was no soft carpet to embrace his feet, only the bare boards, for it was another of Papa's oddities that none of the bedrooms should be carpeted; not even his own.

As he dabbled his hands in the cold water and half-heartedly doused his face, a sudden thought sent a feeling of sensuous delight coursing through his body. Tonight was bath night! Tonight, he would sit, hunched up in the hip-bath, hot water covering his nether limbs while his valet sluiced more hot water over his shoulders. That was one of Mama's oddities; one that he delighted in, ordering that her children should have a bath once a fortnight.

The carriage, jolting and rocking along the rough mud track roads, leading from Germany towards the northern pass into Switzerland, aroused no interest either in the countryside or the small towns through which it passed. Yet had the good folk been able to decipher the faded, chipped gilt coat of arms, they would have been surprised to note that the shabby, decrepit vehicle belonged to none other than His Majesty, King George III of England.

Their surprise would have been even greater could they have seen the two strangely diverse travellers within.

The younger man wore a stern, impassive air, his eyes cold and steady, as staring at his open-mouthed sleeping companion sprawled on the opposite seat, he appeared to be considering the tactics of a military operation. Prince Edward was indeed contemplating how to deal with this newly arisen situation. Having served two years as a cadet in the Hanoverian army, two years during which he had proved himself a first-class soldier, attaining the rank of colonel and winning the praise of all his superiors, his father was now sending him to Geneva to take a further military course, but God in Heaven, how had Papa ever come to choose such a debauched, boorish individual as Baron Wangenheim as his tutor?

His lips tightened. Just as he had chosen to give him the oldest, shabbiest vehicle in the royal coach-house, so he had picked on this man. Edward continued to regard him with disgust, as with a loud snore, the creature awoke sufficiently to undo another button of the tightly strained uniform jacket across his protruding stomach.

For two years he had suffered his harsh discipline, his uncouth manners and his greed, for although the King allowed £6,000 for their mutual maintenance, the Baron only allowed Edward a guinea and a half a week as pocket money.

Thank God he had not drunk or gambled with the other cadets, sons of Prussian aristocrats, otherwise he would have been deeply in debt, but it was galling that he was unable to entertain as the others did. True, he received numerous invitations into aristocratic drawing-rooms, but match-making *mütters* were quickly put in their place by the watchful Wangenheim, who accompanied him everywhere. Over and over again he had written to his father complaining of the Baron's parsimony and of his refusal to allow him the use of the coach or even a horse. The letters had been ignored, as was the request that his valet, Rhymers, should be dismissed, for never was there such a sly, sneaking, tale-telling lackey, reporting his every movement to the Baron.

Edward had now reached a decision. Once they had taken up their abode in Geneva, life was going to be different. Geneva, he had heard, was the accepted place for the finishing off of the education of the high-born of Europe; a stopping-off place for the wild, extravagant youth doing the Grand Tour; a meeting place for bankers, consolidating their wealth, Thomas Coutts, the London banker, was a frequent visitor . . . they were already acquainted and Edward intended meeting him at the first opportunity. Mr. Coutts would be only too willing to advance him a loan, knowing that when he became of age and received his dukedom, there would be a generous government allowance.

Another thought was uppermost in his mind. Not for

much longer would his brothers be able to scoff and call him Simon Pure. He was going to live like a man, not a schoolboy. He would take a mistress and prove his manhood and be damned to the combined watchfulness of the Baron and Rhymers.

.   .   .   .   .

Mademoiselle Thérèse-Bernadine Mongenet, standing by the window watching passers-by picking their steps over the cobbled street, suddenly turned, shrugging her expressive shoulders and with a swish of silk approached her mother's chair, her small oval face clouded with simulated repentance.

'I'm truly sorry, Maman, to be the cause of so much distress, but you must recall, I am no longer a child . . .'

'Exactly so . . . how can I ever forget? My own daughter . . . now twenty-six and still unmarried.'

'Marriage is not all that it is purported to be. It does not guarantee any more happiness than . . .'

'Than the way you live? Seeking admiration from every officer freshly posted to Besançon? Becoming the mistress of first one . . . then another . . .'

'Maman, that is not true. Is it my fault that the gentlemen find me attractive? And I have been the mistress of only one gentleman, the Baron de Fortisson . . .'

'And now that you have found one of higher rank . . . or more wealth, you have decided to transfer your affections . . .'

'There are other reasons, Maman . . .'

'Then why not take a husband? The Holy Mother knows you've had some wonderful offers . . . and there will be more.' Madame Mongenet's voice took on a wheedling tone. 'See what a good marriage your sister Jeanne-Beatrix has made. Will this other . . . this other gentleman offer marriage?'

'I neither know nor care, Maman. At least, he will give me the good life . . .'

'Bah!' There was anger in her voice now. 'Traipsing about the country, like a common camp-follower . . .'

'You are cruel, Maman. Phillipe-Claude is the Marquis de Permangle . . .'

'*Mon Dieu!* A marquis now! Soon you will be too haughty to visit us.' She glanced round the room with slow, cold deliberation; a room that while not vaunting any display of wealth spoke of comfort and good housekeeping.

Impulsively, Thérèse-Bernadine went down on her knees, her voice, caressing and low, 'Never, chère Maman, never. I love you all . . . you, Papa . . . my sister, my brothers . . .'

'Then stay with us. Marry. Give Papa and me some grandchildren. As yet, Jeanne-Beatrix is childless . . .'

She rose to her feet, shaking her head. 'Not for me, Maman. I have decided. The marquis owns several chateaux. Just imagine, Maman, I shall be mistress of a chateau. I shall travel . . . Paris . . . London . . .'

Anger and grief came tumbling out. 'Then go with your marquis . . . after he has bought you from your baron.' She burst into noisy weeping. 'Never did I think a daughter of mine would be the subject of a dispute in a court of law . . . like a prize cow, strayed into his neighbour's pasture . . . and both claiming possession. You are nothing but a . . . a courtesan . . .'

There was hauteur in Thérèse-Bernadine's reply. 'Does it not prove the love the Baron has for me, that he does not wish me to go? Does it not prove that Phillipe-Claude's love is also so strong that he is prepared to pay all costs if he loses the case?'

Her mother was muttering more to herself than addressing her daughter. '. . . the humiliation . . . the disgrace . . . the Baron bringing a case against another man for luring away his mistress . . . and you that woman . . .'

. . . . . .

14

Edward had now been in Geneva for six months. On arrival he had once again remonstrated with the Baron; once again he had written his father. All to no avail.

He had been amazed to find Geneva so full of wealthy people, mostly French aristocrats, who wisely, hearing the distant rumble of revolution, had liquidated their estates and transferred the money to Swiss banks. The streets, theatres and eating houses were packed with French *émigrés*, quick to seek out Edward, fawning on him and, hearing of his pecuniary difficulties, quick to offer a loan, which Edward with equal alacrity accepted.

At first he had attempted to remain incognito, giving himself the title of Le Comte de Hoya, but all too soon, everyone knew his true identity.

He had been fortunate in meeting a certain Major Vilette, a Swiss educated in England, in whom he was able to confide his troubles. Although there was a big difference in their ages, their friendship flourished, the Major readily lending him money and introducing him to Auguste Vas- serot, Baron de Vincy, another Swiss of considerable wealth, who delighted in entertaining the cosmopolitan society.

It was in his salon that Edward met Audeoud, a young man about his own age, who appeared overwhelmed at finding himself in the company of a prince, consequently longing to prove some aspect of his own importance.

'Do you ever go to the theatre, Sir?' he queried.

'In London, yes. I have been on occasion . . .'

'Did you meet any of the actresses . . . intimately?'

'No. I was very young. I was accompanied by my tutors.'

'A pity, Sir, but it can be remedied. I am closely acquainted with several of the ladies at the Comedy Theatre. If you wish, I could arrange a meeting . . .' There was nothing he would like better. George had his Mrs. Robinson; William his Polly Finch; now it was his turn.

Throughout the performance he showed little enthusiasm, wondering all the time as to what type of girl existed behind the paint and make-up, the flimsy, scanty costume and the erotic gyrations of her body, but at last amid thunderous applause. Audeoud was taking his arm and leading him round to the green-room.

It was Edward's first experience of a theatre back-stage, and it came as a shock to him, as amongst the collection of odd pieces of furniture and stage sets, men and women, some in a state of half dress, openly lay around making love. Several of the women invitingly ogled the two young men, but it was on one of the doors that Audeoud knocked and demanded, 'La Duleque, may I come in . . . I have a visitor, Le Comte de Hoya.'

There was a giggle of laughter. 'If you mean Prince Edward—*certainement*—but no other.'

Audeoud held the door open for Edward. A wave of stale perfume, intermixed with perspiration-stained gowns, assailed his nostrils. The girl had her back to him, but he could see through the mirror, as she sat removing the grease-paint . . . a plump-faced girl—a wanton, roguish look in her eye as she called, 'A Prince for La Duleque! *Parbleu!*' and turning round on her stool rose to meet him, her loose wrap falling apart displaying a generous amount of bosom as, throwing her arms around him, she kissed him noisily on both cheeks. 'Welcome, *mon chéri*, welcome!'

Taken aback by such an unorthodox greeting, Edward's first instinct was to flee the room, but Audeoud had already pulled out two stools and the lady opening the door was yelling in a strident voice, 'Monique! Audeoud is here to take you out to supper.'

Just what followed, Edward was never quite sure. His feeling of immature gaucherie, intermixed with acute embarrassment, carried him from one station to another. He was aware of leaving the theatre with La Duleque; of climbing the stairs to her room; of clinging embraces and passionate kisses; his own fumbling, clumsy responses; her teasing laughter, until finally, out of the sour, fetid apartment, his thankfulness to be gulping in the ice-cold air blowing down from the mountains.

He almost laughed aloud. So this was the great thing called love . . . the thing that drove men to distraction. He prayed he would never see La Duleque again . . . but the next day he was climbing those stairs . . . and the next.

.   .   .   .   .

The Baron was feeling indisposed; at least that was the excuse given by his valet when he did not appear for breakfast. Edward smiled wryly. More likely the old curmudgeon was sleeping late, having stayed awake until the early hours of the morning to check the time of his arrival home.

He had thrown all discretion to the wind. He did not care how much Wangenheim knew of his affair with La Duleque. Now, this morning, he was going to have the luxury of breakfasting alone. It was towards the end of the meal that the courier from England was announced, and Edward immediately gave orders that he should be shown into the breakfast-room. It was a new experience for him, to be acting as though he was master of the establishment, and he was determined to make the most of it.

Greetings over, the leather wallet was unlocked and casually, as though it was an everyday task, Edward scanned the letters. Heavens above . . . it was almost unbelievable, but there was actually a letter for him . . . and in his father's scrawling handwriting!

Impatiently he tore it open and began to read. There were several pages of the almost indecipherable scrawl, but certain phrases thrust themselves before his eyes as though in bold print. 'Wicked boy.' 'Sins of the flesh.'

'Loose wanton women.' 'Deliberate, rash extravagance.' But most prominent of all his 'base behaviour towards his loving parents. Away from home, all these years, yet not one letter had they received from him.'

His brain reeled. What did it mean? Then realisation came. Why had he not thought of it before? The Baron had intercepted his letters. Not one had reached his father.

Pushing back his chair, he raced upstairs, bursting into the Baron's room. For a moment he stopped dead as he regarded his tutor, sitting up in bed, night-cap awry on his bald head, breakfast tray in front of him, a piece of steak, dripping with egg-yolk half-way to his mouth, and glaring angrily at the intruder.

'What, Sir, is the meaning of this?' he blustered.

'What, Sir, is the meaning of this?' Edward waved the letter. 'From my father who tells me he has never received a single letter from me. Explain it, Sir!'

The Baron was quite unperturbed and went on eating, pausing between mouthfuls to manage, 'His Majesty's instructions were that under no circumstances was he to be bothered by trivial matters. He placed me *in loco parentis*. Therefore I intercepted your letters; letters full of petty complaints.'

'Petty complaints! That you kept me, a prince of the realm, short of the ordinary pleasures any young gentleman might expect? A miserable allowance of one and a half guineas a week . . . and all the time, my father to think I had never written. By God, Sir, you have much to account for.'

'And you, my cock-a-hoop princeling, for let me tell you, I have already acquainted His Majesty of your infamous loose behaviour . . .'

'So I gathered from his letter . . .' Lost for words, Edward could only emit an exclamation of disgust and stamp from the room.

He didn't care a fig what was done about La Duleque.

He had found out that she was playing him and Audeoud one against the other, and the whole business sickened him.

The Baron wasn't slow to act. Joining forces with Audeoud's parents, they approached the lady, suggesting that she leave Geneva. At first, La Duleque was obstinate. Why should she leave Geneva where she was so popular? But finally, for the sum of twenty louis, she capitulated. While not regretting her departure, Edward was furious that no matter what he did, he was spied and reported upon, and now more than ever, he realised the futility of making any further complaint to his father.

·   ·   ·   ·   ·

La Duleque had gone but Edward was not lonely. He could pick and choose from the salons of the aristocrats or from the numerous brothels, some of which were as lavishly furnished and appointed as any gentleman's town mansion. The stage still had a strange fascination for him and thus it was that his choice of a more or less permanent mistress fell upon an actress, Adelaide Dubos. On borrowed money, he took a small apartment, visiting her whenever possible; a most delightful mode of living compared with Baron Wangenheim's dour, teutonic company.

Then came the rude awakening. Adelaide became pregnant. He was utterly deflated when she told him of his impending fatherhood.

'Are you sure? Really sure?' he stammered. She shrugged her shoulders and gesticulated with upturned palms. 'As sure as a woman can be.'

'But what will you do?' He had thought himself so manly. Now he realised his ignorance and his immaturity.

'More to the point,' came the tart rejoinder, 'what are *you* going to do?'

He tried to think. George and Fred and William had all

faced up to this same predicament. Should he write and ask their advice? No, they would only laugh and deride him. Of course she must be provided for. That was the honourable thing to do. He groaned inwardly, wondering where the money would come from.

'You will, of course, stay on in this apartment and I will arrange for you to have a regular allowance . . .

'. . . and the child?'

'I will have a settlement drawn up . . .'

She sighed. 'I am truly sorry, Sir, that this has happened. Perhaps I could arrange an abortion . . .'

'Most certainly not! I would not have you risk your life at the filthy hands of some old crone or quack. I will see to it both you and the child have adequate attention. *Have you as yet told anyone else?*'

'Only my sister, Victoire . . .'

'Then swear her to secrecy and tell no-one. We have been most discreet about our friendship. Let the discretion continue. If my father was to hear of it, it might be difficult to get the money.' As an after-thought, he added warningly, 'He might also move me from Geneva and we would neither of us wish that to happen, would we?'

Yet by the time came for Adelaide to give up her stage engagements, all Geneva knew the reason and many guessed the paternity. Oddly enough, Edward had developed a closer relationship with the girl. To begin with, she was much more lady-like than La Duleque and the thought that she was carrying his child stirred him in a strange way. He was not in love with her but where before she had been a mere plaything, a pleasant little creature to fulfil his physical needs and an attractive companion at the same time, now she was a dear friend in need of comfort and care. As the months progressed, he found pleasure in going to the apartment just to share a well-cooked, tête-à-tête meal; to sing to the accompaniment of her guitar; to teach her English, an entertainment that always ended in a riot of laughter.

. . . . .

The year was coming to a close. Soon it would be Christmas. Edward thought nostalgically of England and home, recalling the lavish entertainments held at the Queen's House; the huge, decorated yew tree in the drawing-room; an innovation brought over from Germany by his mother as a young bride. Every house in London would be lit up, flinging wide its double doors in an effort as to who could entertain on the most brilliant scale. The Prince of Wales would be outdoing them all with extravagant, gay mad frolics at Carlton House, while he . . . he wouldn't even have the pleasure of Adelaide's company for the child was expected round about Christmas. He would be glad when it was all over, for of recent weeks she had been miserable, tired and listless. His visits had been fewer, and they only from a sense of duty, for there was no pleasure in listening to her continuous moanings about her present dreary existence and her determination to go back to the stage at the earliest opportunity.

The festive season was already in full swing in Geneva and Edward did not lack for invitations, all of which he accepted with alacrity in an effort to dispel his own gloom. Yet his pleasure was always accompanied by a sense of guilt for he was generous enough to concede that the woman always carried the heavier share of the burden. Yet was that not Nature's plan? Why, his mother, Her Majesty the Queen, had undergone the ordeal, fifteen times.

. . . . .

He had given orders that he was not to be awakened. He would ring when he was ready for his breakfast. Last night's ball had gone on until the early hours of the morning and then he had escorted home one of the professional dancers who had entertained the assembly; a most provocative little creature who knew how to tempt a man; a wanton little slut if ever there was one. He would spend the morning in bed and then call on Adelaide in the afternoon for he had not seen her for almost a week.

He was awakened by someone shaking his shoulder. Curse the man. Hadn't he given orders not to be disturbed? He was fully awake now, cursing as though he was on the barrack square.

'Sir . . . Sir . . .' the man kept interrupting.

'Well, what is it, now that you've got me awake?'

'Sir. There is a lady downstairs. She will not go away without seeing you . . .'

A lady? His bemused mind tried to think. The girl he was with last night? No. She would not dare. Then it struck him with such clarity that it was as though Adelaide was in the room with him.

He was out of bed, his man reaching for his master's morning-robe as he demanded, 'The lady's name?'

'She would not give it, Sir.'

Of course she would not. If it was a message from Adelaide she would be more discreet than usual, especially if it was the message he was hoping for . . . that the baby had arrived.

As he entered the breakfast room, a woman rose to greet him, throwing back her heavy black veil. It was Victoire, Adelaide's sister. Panic rose within him. He did not need to be told what had happened. Putting her gently back into the chair, he whispered, 'Tell me . . . how . . . why . . . why did it happen?'

'She was in labour all day yesterday. The child was born last night. A difficult labour . . . earlier than we expected but Adelaide was in good spirits all the time. Then a

22

haemorrhage . . . and before we were hardly aware of it, she was gone.'

Now that she had delivered her message she was free to liberate her tears. Edward, too, was so overcome that a silence fell between them save for his muttered, 'My poor little Adelaide . . . My poor little *liebling* . . .' until as though suddenly remembering, he demanded, 'The baby?'

'A little girl . . . a fine, healthy child.'

He rang the bell and ordered coffee to be taken to his room, '. . . and refreshments for the lady . . . whatever she asks . . . and my carriage within the half-hour.'

His carriage. His latest extravagance. But what other prince was there in the whole of Christendom who didn't own a carriage? Bought with borrowed money, of course. No-one could buy a carriage on an income of a guinea-and-a-half a week. He pulled himself together. Why was he thinking of such mundane matters when a lovely young girl lay dead and he was responsible for her death? Anything . . . anything to stop him thinking of that small still form . . . but he must go and pay his last respects.

They drove to the apartment in complete silence. He did not know what to say. He had never anticipated this outcome. Adelaide had had the best medical attention; the best midwife. Then why?

He stared down at the little figure in her white gown, her face completely relaxed, almost smiling as she did when welcoming him for the evening. No more pleasant interludes of kisses and caresses. She was gone and he had no mind at that moment to replace her. He was horrified to recall that last night, as she lay dying, he had another woman in his arms. Blinded by tears, he stumbled away, then, as a piercing, sharp wail came from the next room, he stopped.

'The baby?'

He followed Victoire and watched her lift the bundle

23

from the cot, straightening its shawl before holding it out to him.'

'Your daughter, Sir.'

For a moment he quailed. He couldn't handle anything so tiny and fragile but the moment of trepidation passed and as he cradled it in a firm grip, the wailing ceased and the red-faced scrap of humanity opened its eyes. Edward had never truly loved Adelaide in the sense of really belonging, but in that moment, he knew that he loved his daughter. Handing her back to her aunt, he said brokenly, 'Look after her . . . You will be paid well. As for the funeral, spare no expense. I will meet the bills.'

He made his way out to the waiting carriage, one glimmer of hope in the midst of all the sorrow; someone of his own to love and cherish, but it must be kept secret. He dreaded the thought it might become public knowledge he was the father of a bastard child. Let them guess and talk but never let them have proof by his vaunting and showing off the child.

•　　•　　•　　•　　•

It was the most miserable Christmas he had ever spent; still accepting invitations; putting on a façade of enjoyment and goodwill, while deep down he was wretched and despondent. A settlement had been drawn up to ensure his daughter's future; payment for Aunt Victoire to act as her nurse, but Aunt Victoire was already objecting, saying she preferred the stage. That meant the child would have to be fostered. They had already decided the baby should be called Adelaide Victoire Auguste, Edward insisting that she should be brought up in the Protestant faith. But where was the money to come from? There was only one thing to do. He must go home to England; get away without Wangenheim's knowledge . . .

•　　•　　•　　•　　•

God and Mr. Sturt be thanked they had arrived in London. Through blizzard and fog they had sped across the Continent, Mr. Sturt apparently cognisant with all its roads. Of course, it was ridiculous to make the journey in January, the worst month of the year, but he had reached the point when he could no longer tolerate the Baron nor his debts nor his father's indifference. Vasserot and Major Vilette had organised the flight . . . fresh horses at this inn . . . a bed and a meal at that. . . .

The slow crawl of the mail-coach, led by men with lighted flambeaux, had perhaps been the most frustrating part of the whole journey. But London at last. He was home.

Under the style of Major Armstrong, a room at Nerot's Hotel in James Street had been booked for him, and giving orders that he was not to be disturbed in the morning, he lost no time in retiring. His plans were already made. He was going to seek the help and advice of his brother, the Prince of Wales, but aware of George's indolent mode of life, knew that it would be of little use calling at Carlton House before noon. Yet despite the comfort of the feather-bed and the ministrations of the maid with her warming pan upon the fresh-smelling sheets, sleep refused to come, his brain being a seething mass of excitement. He groaned aloud as he recalled that he had left Geneva owing £20,000. Would his father settle his debts, in addition to giving him an allowance? It wasn't only his financial position that irked him. He wanted proper recognition : not a schoolboy, afraid of his father and tutor. His brother, Frederick, had been created Duke of York when he was twenty-one . . . He was now in his twenty-third year. Why the difference?

How should he approach his father? Time and again he composed an opening gambit, only to discard it the next moment, until weary and exhausted, he finally decided to be advised by George, and fell into a troubled sleep, only to dream of an angry, violent, demented father.

By the time he was ready to call on his brother, the thin January sun had taken the place of the fog, and with rising spirits Edward decided to walk, rather than call a carriage. It was good to be walking the London streets again.

As he entered the richly carpeted hall of Carlton House, he noticed with envy the new furnishings and pictures, everything in such excellent taste, that there and then he made an inward vow. One day, perhaps not too far away, he would have an establishment that would outshine his brother's for luxury and culture.

He suddenly wondered whether his brother would be alone or would Mrs. Fitzherbert be there? He had never met the lady; all he knew was the gossip of the Geneva salons. Had George really married her? Not that it mattered if he had; the Royal Marriage Act ruled out its recognition, but rumour had it his brother was her adoring slave, and she a twice-widowed lady.

A roar of boisterous surprise greeted the flunkey's announcement, George striding over to the door to greet him. 'Edward, God Almighty, what are you doing here?' But the next moment he was being warmly embraced by George and then by Frederick.

'Come, sit down. Brandy or Madeira?' He handed over a brimming glass of brandy.

'Ah . . . no, George . . . not at this early hour. I prefer Madeira . . .'

'Still the good-living boy . . . eh?' Another boisterous laugh, as he handed a glass to Frederick and refilled his own. 'And now, tell us, how and why are you here?'

'Yes, tell us why.' Frederick's drawling voice held amusement. 'Running away from a lady? We've heard of your numerous peccadilloes . . . Is she demanding recompense, and you've come to ask Papa to help you out . . . ?'

'If so, dear brother, you're doomed to disappointment . . .'

Edward felt a surge of anger at his brothers' levity, but he needed their help and advice and so controlled his temper.

'Nothing of the kind . . . my dealings with the ladies have always been beyond reproach.'

George threw his arms around Frederick, both unable to restrain their mirth.

'What about the little French actress? We heard all about her . . .'

Edward was aware of a sense of utter futility. 'So you know?'

'My dear brother, all London knows, including His Majesty, our dear father. But come, don't look so blue-devilled about it all, if it's advice about women you've come about you couldn't have consulted more expert . . .'

'It's not about women.' Edward couldn't stem his rising irritation. 'I've come . . . unknown to either my father or my tutor back in Geneva . . . to ask for justice. My father allows Baron Wangenheim £6,000 a year for our joint maintenance. How much do you think the Baron doles out to me? One and a half guineas a week! How much do you spend in a week?'

Having now started to list his grievances and finding an interested audience, Edward went on and on, recounting the whole story of the Baron's greed and the interception of his letters resulting in the King's wrongful impression of his filial neglect.

George and Frederick, forced into silence, listened with apparent passivity but when Edward, coming to the end of his story, paused for breath, it was George who interrupted, with forcible sincerity, 'But it's damnable that you should have been treated like this. We'll go along to see His Majesty this very afternoon . . .'

'If he will see us,' came Frederick's laconic drawl . . .

'But surely,' began Edward, 'his own sons . . .'

'You forget, dear brother, that you're dealing with a madman . . .'

'But . . . he is not so . . . so disturbed that he cannot meet me?'

'No? Wait until you see him, the great blubbering, dribbling lunatic, never properly dressed, going around in a dirty old morning robe; never allowing his barber to touch his hair or beard . . .'

'Slobbering over our sisters, stroking their hair. It's almost obscene to watch him.'

Edward listened in amazement. That these two elder brothers, always regarded as their parents' golden boys, should speak of their sick father with such callousness, filled him with repugnance.

George's voice was rising in anger. 'Last year, I thought the Regency was in my grasp. He had reached such a pitch of madness, that he had to be put in a strait-jacket and locked in his room. The Regency Bill was drawn up, just needed the necessary signatures, when dear Papa takes a turn for the better . . .' He broke off to throw himself into a chair with a gesture of violence before continuing, 'Then to add insult to injury, a thanksgiving service for His Majesty's recovery was held at the Abbey, and along with the others, I had to go and give my thanks to God, when all the time I was cursing my ill-luck.' He suddenly adopted a lighter tone. 'And now, dear brother, your coming could be a veritable godsend . . .'

'A godsend?'

'To provoke the old fool. You are going to stay here at Carlton House with us. That and the knowledge that we are on your side will rile him . . .'

From the hall came the deep, booming sound of a gong. 'Ah, lunch. Now, Edward, I have a treat for you. You shall meet my angel wife, Maria. She, too, will enjoy the surprise . . . and then away to meet our beloved parents . . .

but will they enjoy the surprise . . . eh, Fred . . . ?' and the
two indulged in another bout of raucous laughter.

.   .   .   .   .

The visit to the Queen's House was a dismal failure. It
was only after a long wait that the King condescended to
see the Prince of Wales and then so great was his fury on
hearing of Edward's unlawful home-coming, that George
was glad to make his escape, lest his father should attack
him as he had done on a previous occasion.

Aware of Edward's dejection, he quickly arranged a
party for that night, but Edward was no great gambler or
drinker, and his brother's efforts only served to make him
more wretched. That George could live in such luxury
and spend with such liberty . . . it was grossly unfair.

He felt an instant liking for Maria Fitzherbert. As though
she sensed he was in some kind of trouble, she made conversation easy for him, asking about people and places in
Geneva, knowing the city well, having travelled exten-
sively on the Continent. George had already told her of his
brother's dash to England and she was all womanly sympathy. 'Money is a curse, Sir. No matter how much you
have, you still need more. Take George, for instance. His
allowance is enormous . . . yet so are his debts.'

It was obvious she had George's well-being at heart, for
several times throughout the evening she endeavoured to
curb his drinking only to be answered by curt rudeness.

Despair, anger, bitterness overwhelmed him, as day after
day, he called on the King, waiting hour after hour in a
small ante-chamber in the hope that his father might deign
to see him . . . all to no avail. Night after night, George
and Frederick indulged in their riotous assemblies. If Mrs.
Fitzherbert was present and saw that the horse-play was
getting out of hand, she quickly begged leave to depart.
Edward was now experiencing an exaggerated mode of

living and he began to loathe it as much as his penurious style with Wangenheim. Wait, only wait until he had his own establishment. There would be luxury . . . even ostentation . . . but it would be ostentation with dignity.

He had been in London a fortnight, when a note was delivered to him stating His Majesty had enrolled his son, Prince Edward, into the army with the rank of Colonel, and that he was being posted to Gibraltar.

The three brothers were stunned. Then George and Frederick began shouting and cursing at their father's infamous behaviour. Only Edward remained silent. Gibraltar. His allowance? His dukedom? He must speak to his father. His insistence finally won. His father would see him on the morning he was due to sail, but when Edward was ushered into the royal presence, his speech deserted him, so shocked was he at his father's unkempt, wild appearance.

His brothers' description had not been exaggerated. Under the mane of unkempt hair, his unshaved cheeks showed bruises as though he had fallen or been struck. He was obviously in a very weak state, his hands trembling violently, and his head rolling from side to side. No wonder, thought Edward pityingly, considering all the purging and bleeding he had undergone. Overwhelming compassion submerged his anger. All the protests were left unsaid. There was no demonstration of affection on either side; neither were there any recriminations. After ten minutes of fruitless, blatant platitudes and indiscernible mumblings, Edward bowed himself out, unsure whether the King had dismissed him, or whether he himself had curtailed the interview. No mention of his dukedom, his allowance or settlement of his debts had been made.

George and Frederick had greeted his account with derision. More fool him for not shouting the old man down and demanding his rights. They were beginning to tire of Edward's company. He was a bit of a bore; too virtuous for their liking, but they offered to drive down to Portsmouth with him to see him aboard the frigate *Southampton*.

There, a pleasant surprise awaited him, the citizens turning out in their thousands to welcome him. After two days of sightseeing and civic entertainments, the *Southampton* sailed to the fluttering of bunting, and the sound of naval bands intermingling with the booming of guns. Edward felt his spirits rising. He was going to a new life, free from the tyranny of the Baron. In his place he was to have the company of Captain Charles Crauford, formerly an aide-de-camp to his brother the Duke of York and now, as they sailed to Gibraltar, fast becoming his friend.

2

A loyal welcome, almost equal to his send-off, greeted Edward at Gibraltar, General Charles O'Hara, Commander of the Garrison, awaiting him on the quay-side, with troops of the Queen's Royal Regiment on parade and lining the route to the General's residence where Edward was to stay until he was settled in an establishment of his own.

As he passed along the lines of men he found it difficult to hide his contempt and disdain, their general turnout was so slovenly, from their dress to their movements. 'Only wait,' he thought, his gorge rising, 'only wait until I begin to discipline them.' He would enjoy the task until each and every one of them fitted perfectly into the military machine.

General O'Hara, overwhelmed at the honour of having the King's son under his roof, spared no energy or expense to entertain his guest. Balls and levées were the order of the day, all the society on the Rock, both military and civilian, being invited to meet Edward. The civilians were a motley crowd of many races, fawning on him, almost ready to lick his boots in their efforts to ingratiate themselves.

Though he might be Prince Charming in the ballroom, when daylight came, he was Colonel Guelph on garrison duty every other day; days that were marked by extra early morning parades and long hours of drilling. Consequently, he was none too popular either with the troops or the officers unaccustomed to early rising.

Edward, however, was unrelenting. He had now found

a small house and with Captain Crauford's assistance and advice was fitting it out and discovering the £500 allowed was far from being sufficient to compromise with his taste.

Yet when the house was ready for occupation he found himself more lonely than he had ever been in his life before. He had made no friends among the junior officers; they were too resentful about his mode of discipline and as for the ladies, they were in a minority on the Rock. Of course, there were a few hopeful designing mamas; numerous scheming wives, making it all too clear that they were willing to be the most discreet of mistresses.

As in Geneva, Gibraltar boasted a thriving business in prostitution. There were times when, in his loneliness and frustration, he resorted to a brothel, only to hate and despise himself afterwards. How he longed to have another mistress like Adelaide.

Then the idea came to him. Why not invite her sister Victoire to come over and join him, bringing the baby with her? The thought of seeing the baby again excited him. He had visited them before fleeing Geneva and had marvelled at the change in the baby in so short a time. Gone was the little red, angry-looking, puckered face and in its place a wide-eyed cherub. It would be wonderful to watch his daughter grow up.

No sooner had he conceived the idea than it must be put into operation. Taking his valet, Moré, into his confidence the man was sent off to Geneva to bring Mlle. Victoire Dubos and the baby.

To fill in the waiting time, he looked around for a suitable apartment and having found it, delighted in fitting up a nursery. They would have to be discreet. Victoire could be a widow with her small daughter . . . he a dear friend occasionally visiting her. Would she be as accommodating as Adelaide? As gentle and compliant?

In the meantime, Captain Crauford had been replaced by Colonel Symes who was aghast to find Edward was already in debt, despite his Colonel's pay of £5,000, and began to look around to see where the money was going.

At last the day of Victoire's arrival. That morning, the troops were dismissed at an earlier hour than they had ever before known, for Edward received information the ship was off the Rock and by now must have entered the harbour and disembarked her passengers.

He entered his house with a light step and jubilation in his heart. The longing and loneliness were over. Moré, awaiting him, was hovering about in the hall.

He siezed the man by both arms. 'At last, Moré. Thank you a thousand times. Where have you put the lady? In the library?'

He strode across to the room, flinging open the door in eager anticipation. Victoire Dubos rose and curtsied, her face expressionless. His fleeting impression was that she was nowhere near as pretty a girl as Adelaide. There was something uneasy about her dumb blank face. He looked around and then demanded, 'The baby? Where is she?'

'Dead.'

'Dead? How? What happened?'

'She died at sea. On our way here.' Her voice was as toneless as her face was blank. 'She was buried at sea.'

He was lost for words. All his happy anticipation lay at the bottom of the Mediterranean. It was Victoire who broke the silence, almost shouting in a shrill voice, 'You are not holding me to blame, are you?'

'How did it come about?'

'A baby of six months is a delicate creature, Sir. The travelling upset her. She was sick . . .' She lifted her shoulders in resignation. There was nothing more that she could tell him.

'You must excuse me, Ma'am. I have just come from the barrack square. I will have a meal sent in to you and then later we can talk and I will take you to your apartment.'

. . . . .

34

Perhaps it was the death of the baby that doomed their friendship from the beginning but Victoire was no easy conquest as Adelaide had been.

Sometimes she would lead Edward on to believe she was willing for love-making only to stop him when desire was mounting within him. When he angrily accused her of being frigid, she laughed in his face. 'But a girl has to be cautious, Sir. If my sister had been more cautious, she would have been alive today.'

Soon she was complaining of boredom. Save for his visits, which under the circumstances quickly became less frequent, she saw no-one but the maid Edward had engaged for her. Edward was full of sympathy and when she announced she had a theatrical engagement awaiting her in Marseilles, he was only too ready to make arrangements for her passage.

Within a few days of her departure, Colonel Symes diffidently broached the subject. 'I . . . I am delighted, Sir, that you have parted with the lady . . .'

Edward stared in stupefaction. How much did Symes know?

'Perhaps you will explain more clearly,' he began haughtily.

'We were all well aware, Sir, of your relationship with the lady, none more than I, with the unenviable task of reporting to His Majesty all your movements . . .'

'The devil you have!'

'Exactly, Sir. I agree with your sentiments but now that she has gone I do beg of you, Sir, not to repeat the . . . the . . . er affair . . .'

'Then what do you suggest I should do to relieve the tedium of this God-forsaken place?' Edward's voice was cold and hard.

'Well, Sir . . . the other officers . . .'

'Many of them are openly living with mistresses. Others are enjoying their brother officers' wives . . .'

'I agree, Sir. I agree. But you are the son of His Majesty.'

'I am still a man for all that! I ask you again. What should I do?'

Colonel Symes, flustered and embarrassed, could only stare down at his highly polished boots. Then without lifting his eyes, 'There are several excellent brothels, Sir, establishments specially run for the military . . .'

'Save your breath, Colonel. I am no lover of the bawdy-house. Neither will you persuade me against taking a mistress when I so desire,' and turning on his heel, left the discomforted gentleman.

The humiliation of it all. That he should be spied upon and his every action reported. He had thought he had been so discreet about Victoire. He almost laughed aloud as he recalled with irony the paucity of what had happened between them. But, by God, he swore to himself, it would be different next time. No more hole in the corner business for him. He would live openly with his next mistress and be damned to them all.

.   .   .   .   .

It was early Autumn before the 7th Regiment of Foot, his own regiment, arrived at the garrison. Edward felt the sense of excitement surging within him. A challenge. These men were his material to mould as he had been trained to mould men.

He watched them come ashore, his excitement turning to anger and disgust. Never before had he seen such rag-taggle effigies of soldiers; such slovenly, unkempt, burlesque caricatures. In the short time he had been on the Rock, he had, despite the criticism of his fellow officers, brought about a certain measure of discipline to the Queen's. Now to see these troops so obviously lacking in training filled him with a furious determination. No time must be lost. Immediate action was called for. That night,

36

on his orders, the newly arrived troops were confined to barracks. As they lay on their palliasses in the unhygienic, insanitary barracks they ranted and raved and cursed Edward's very existence. They had been at sea for three weeks; three weeks during which they had indulged in much bawdy, lewd talk of how they would spend their first night in Gibraltar. They had heard much of the wine-shops and the eager, willing light-skirts and now, because His Royal Highness had faulted their parade on the quay-side . . . Hell and damnation take him.

      •   •   •   •   •

The brutal, Prussian training was in full swing. Never before had a regiment been subjected to such early morning parades; such rigorous drilling; such detailed inspections; such vicious, sadistic punishments for even minor breaches of discipline . . . even minor breaches of dress.

Never a day went by without a batch of wretched men being strapped to the triangle; their backs bare to receive as many lashes as His Royal Highness decreed; and His Royal Highness took great satisfaction in heavy punishment . . . it was necessary, he sternly maintained, if the men were to be properly disciplined.

When the newly arrived officers complained about the early morning parades, he was quick to point out that he himself was always present as an example to the men. How then could any of them be excused?

They listened to him on parade, shouting, ranting, raving, cursing and roaring like a wild animal, treating the men as though they lacked all privileges of humanity.

They listened to him in the evening, talking over their wine in the mess; chatting and dancing with their wives at this assembly or that; and in bewilderment asked one another, 'How can it be the same man?'

And in the miserable gloomy barracks, men stretched

out on their bellies, attempting to find ease for their lacerated, bleeding backs.

· · · · ·

Edward was growing more dejected. The climate of the Rock did not suit him. He appealed to Colonel Symes that he should make representations to his father to get him moved to somewhere more congenial; somewhere where there were more people, for as yet he had found no-one suitable as a mistress. It was at one of General O'Hara's assemblies that he met Monsieur Fontiny, whose business took him all over the Continent.

In an all male company the conversation naturally turned to the topic of women; Edward's contribution being concerned with the lack of ladies on the Rock. M. Fontiny was all sympathy. What the Prince needed was a lady from his country. French women were superb . . . outstanding . . . so feminine . . . so provocative . . .

Edward laughed as M. Fontiny continued to extol his country-women's rare qualities. 'You tantalise me, Sir. How about finding such a companion for me.'

'Willingly, Sir. Willingly. I am due to visit Marseilles shortly, a city boasting many beautiful ladies. Have you any outstanding abilities that you seek?'

Edward considered for a moment. 'Not really, beyond that she must be a lady. I desire that she shall live with me . . .' He repeated the words, looking M. Fontiny straight in the eye, 'Live with me as my wife. Naturally, she must be pleasing in appearance . . . I would appreciate it if she was musical . . . have good taste in dress . . . Am I asking too much?'

M. Fontiny gave him a wry smile. 'I shall not dare submit any lady's name to you unless she meets all your requirements.'

· · · ·

Thérèse-Bernadine Mongenet and Phillipe-Claude, Marquis de Permangle looked around the small shabby bedroom into which the hotel lackey had shown them.

Phillipe-Claude made a mock courtly bow. 'A thousand pardons, Madame, that the setting for our parting should be so beggarly ...'

'Sh ... Sir, if anyone should hear your remarks ...'

'... and you too, Citoyenne Mongenet, calling me Sir ...'

'I crave your pardon, Citoyen Claude.' She sighed deeply as she seated herself on the sagging bed with its grubby soiled covers, 'Where will you go, Phillipe?'

'Spain. I have just about enough money to get me there.'

'But surely, now that they have taken all your estates you should be safe.'

'There is still my life and they would not hesitate to take that if someone should denounce me on some trumped-up charge. That is why, apart from the fact I have no money on which to maintain you, you are in equal danger so long as you remain in my company.'

'But what will you do in Spain?'

'Find employment of some description, but more to the point, *ma petite*, what will you do? I would urge you to return home to Besançon.'

She shook her head. 'No. The garrison there is now in the hands of the Revolutionary forces. I am well known in Besançon ... as is my acquaintance with you. No, Besançon would be dangerous for me.'

'Then where? I cannot leave you here in Marseilles, alone, friendless ...'

'Why not? I am almost thirty years of age, fully capable of looking after myself ...'

'But you have no money ...'

'I have been considering seeking a theatrical engagement ...'

'*Bon Dieu!*'

She laughed merrily. 'Better to sing than to starve. Now

39

you wish to see about a passage to Malaga and I would examine the theatres of Marseilles. Let us get out of this flea-infested room.'

Together they walked along the streets towards the docks, talking but little lest their cultured speech should betray them as loathed aristocrats, both lost in their own thoughts.

'Permangle!'

As though shot, they spun round seeking the hailing voice not knowing whether to run or hold their ground.

'*Par ma barbe!*' The newcomer had seized Phillipe by the arm and was kissing him demonstratively.

'Fontiny!' Quickly he disengaged himself. 'Not here, my friend. Surely you know better . . .'

'It was the surprise of seeing you . . . and Madame. Alas, I suppose I must then not dare to kiss her hand . . .'

' 'Twould be wiser not to.' Thérèse-Bernadine smiled at M. Fontiny. 'Citoyenne Mongenet is not accustomed to such gallantries.'

'We must talk, since it is so long since we last met. I am on my way to study the sailings for Malaga . . .'

'An odd coincidence, Fontiny, for that is our errand too . . .'

'*Merveilleux!* Then we can all journey together. What an unexpected pleasure!'

'I regret to disappoint you, but Madame is remaining in Marseilles . . .'

'So?' M. Fontiny's eyebrows went up in surprise.

' 'Tis a sad turn of events but unavoidable . . .'

M. Fontiny's brain suddenly became alert to the situation. Why, here was the very lady suitable for His Royal Highness, Prince Edward. She had all the attributes the Prince requested . . . and most important of all she was about to part from her protector. He must find out more.

He took the arms of his companions bringing them to

a halt on the narrow footpath. 'Listen. I have a proposition I would put to you. A proposition that would
smooth out the difficulties for both of you. Let us go back
to my hotel where we can talk.'

'But the sailings? Malaga?'

'All part of my proposition . . . but not today. Come.'

He lost no time in explaining his commission. A certain young English gentleman, an army officer of high
rank, is desirous of finding a lady to be his constant companion. She must be accustomed to associating with the
well-born, to sit by his side at the head of his table . . .

'. . . and to sleep in his bed,' interposed Thérèse.

M. Fontiny bowed significantly but made no comment,
turning to Phillipe to continue, 'I will write to the Prince
tonight . . .'

'Prince!' The ejaculation from both his listeners left an
embarrassing silence.

'I did not intend telling of his rank until . . . until I heard
whether . . . whether . . .'

'. . . I was suitable. May we know the name of the prince,
M. Fontiny?'

'Certainement. He is Prince Edward, fourth son of His
Majesty King George of England.'

It was Thérèse who broke the silence that fell between
them, smiling at them with a whimsical light in her eye.
'I doubt that he will be any different from other men.'
She eyed Phillipe roguishly. '. . . Capricious . . . moody
. . . amorous . . .'

Her light-heartedness relieved the tension. 'So you are
agreeable, Madame, that I write His Highness . . .'

She shrugged her shoulders. 'If you think I would be
acceptable.' She turned to Phillipe with a sudden tenderness, resting her hand on his, 'And you my friend. What
do you think?'

His voice was full of emotion. 'Go to this prince, ma
petite. During the years we have been together, you have

given me great happiness. Now that I am penniless and my life in constant danger it would give me great satisfaction to know you were safe and comfortable.' He turned to M. Fontiny. 'In the meantime, what do you propose we do?'

'We will all sail together for Malaga, to await the Prince's reply.'

Thérèse-Bernadine allowed her mind to wander while the gentlemen continued to talk. Every now and again she caught an odd word . . . even-tempered . . . witty . . . complacent . . . gay . . . a mind of her own. Obviously they were talking about her. She supposed she was complacent but by no means submissive. She had had no serious quarrels with either the Baron de Fortisson or the Marquis de Permangle and saw no reason why she should not be on amicable terms with the Prince. A prince. Vividly, her mother's words came back to her. She was stepping up still higher . . . handed on like a prize cow.

Still, there was one advantage of being a mistress, rather than a wife. If the creature proved unbearable, she could always walk out.

.   .   .   .   .

Edward was endeavouring to subdue his excitement, for after the disappointing, harrowing visit of Victoire he was determined to be prepared for any eventuality.

Mlle. Thérèse-Bernadine was due to arrive any time now. He had sent his personal servant, Beck, to escort her from Malaga, and now his carriage was awaiting them at the quay-side.

M. Fontiny's first letter had caused him a little doubt. The lady, he wrote enthusiastically, was very beautiful, full of charm, gay, witty . . . and musical . . . and approaching thirty years of age. Seven years older than himself, he mused. There was always the danger she might be a domineering spinster. Nevertheless, he had written her, describing life on the Rock, emphasising she must not expect luxury in a military garrison. Her reply had been one of enchantment, sending Edward's hopes soaring high.

The sound of the carriage on the gravel drive brought him to his feet and over to the window. He watched her alight. Slim, graceful and smiling with jet-black curls escaping beneath the brim of her straw bonnet, some to hang provocatively over her shoulder. Then she was being announced.

She sank into a curtsey and as he raised her he was able to look her full in the face. She smiled and in that instant he was lost; it was a smile of such deep warmth and friendship. He found he was still holding her hand as he led her across the room; then helping her to remove the green, silk cloak and holding out a chair.

'I will ring for tea, Ma'am. You must be exhausted after the trip from Malaga . . .'

She regarded him with frank amazement. 'You speak my language, Sir . . . and with such exquisite finesse, while my English, alas, is deplorable.'

He laughed. 'My education was very thorough, Ma'am. French . . . German . . . Italian . . . As for your English, you will, I am sure, be an adept pupil.'

As they talked, he became more and more bemused. She was a witch, casting a spell over him. A beautiful, laughing witch. He was glad when she went up to her room, glad of the respite to muster his strange feelings.

⋅ ⋅ ⋅ ⋅ ⋅

Thérèse-Bernadine took a long, cool look round the bedroom; a man's room, despite the lady's dressing-table which was so obviously new. Cautiously, she opened the adjoining door, to be met by the unperturbed smile of Beck, putting out his master's evening clothes.

43

Thérèse grinned amiably. 'You are soon to your duties, Monsieur Beck.'

'Why, yes, Madame. His Highness honours me by preferring my service to that of others.'

She glanced at the narrow iron bedstead and with the familiarity of their acquaintance asked, 'Does His Highness sleep in that box of a bed?'

' 'Tis a new addition, Madame, since I have been away from Gibraltar.' Was it amusement or sarcasm that she detected in his voice?

She closed the door quietly and removing her dress, decided to take a rest on the big, comfortable looking bed. Would she find contentment with this strange man, this prince, who seemingly had little to say and certainly no pretty speech? Yet he was so delightfully masculine . . . such height . . . the most captivating blond hair and blue eyes. She herself was easy-going, willing to acquiesce . . . well, nearly always. Judging by the money he had sent for her new wardrobe, he was generous, but there, a lady could never truly discern a man's motives. Perhaps his generosity was mere bait.

What would he be like as a lover? She had tried to draw Beck as to the Prince's previous amours, but like the good servant he was, he refused to talk beyond saying he had only been in His Highness' service but a short while and during that time he knew of no lady.

Not that his previous affairs bothered her. Indeed it was better that he was experienced, then they both started level; she with her baron and marquis; he with . . . she cared not who.

. . . . .

They dined tête-à-tête. Thérèse-Bernadine wearing a low-cut dinner gown of the latest mode. Obviously the lady had excellent taste. How much allowance should he sug-

44

gest? As the meal progressed he decided she was a desirable table-companion . . . not a chatter-box, yet always ready with a reply to his stilted attempts at conversation. He was glad that she drank but little wine; he had no liking for ladies who aped their men-folk when the decanter was being passed round.

She sang for him in a sweet, modulated clear voice. He was entranced. How fortunate he had been. How proud he was going to be with her at the head of his dining-table; to entertain his guests . . . and when they had taken their departure . . . to enjoy her nearness.

Yet as the evening sped by, he began to have disturbing doubts. The conviction was growing that here there was no woman on whom he could force himself. He could not invade the privacy of her room . . . his room which he had placed at her disposal. Perhaps it would have been better if he had taken an apartment for her. It was maddening. No other woman had ever so affected him. Was this that rare, much vaunted state called love?

There was a hint of curtness in his voice as he stood up. 'Rising at the crack of dawn, Madame, I retire early. You too have had an arduous day.'

She flashed him a smile, not being sure of the implication of his statement 'Then I will say, "*bon nuit*", Monsieur . . .'

He took her hand and kissed it, gravely replying, '. . . or as we English say, "Good night, Madame".'

She went up the staircase slowly, wondering as to whether the Prince intended visiting her that night. He had given no indication; indeed his mind seemed far away, as though pondering over a problem.

As she undressed she could hear him moving about in his dressing-room. She chose a filmy, lacy *robe-de-nuit* and loosened her curls. For a long time she lay awake, wondering, perplexed, recalling snatches of their conversation. She must consider herself mistress of the house. Did he mean that she was to be some kind of glorified housekeeper? No, not that, for he had instructed her to find herself a trustworthy, personal maid. His carriage was at her disposal. She must buy more clothes. He himself would select jewellery for her. By the time they had finished the meal he had emerged a little from behind that wall of pomp and dignity and she had discovered a boyish, friendly human being. Apparently, he did not intend to rush their relationship, but *Mon Dieu*, this was the first time a man had denied himself the opportunity of bedding with her.

. . ■ ■ . .

Edward, in the next room, was vainly searching for comfort in the narrow truckle-bed. He was a fool, he told himself, when behind that door there was the softness of a goose-feather bed . . . and the softness of an adorable woman. What was holding him back? If he had truly fallen in love with her, surely that knowledge should send him swiftly into her room, but for the life of him he could not pluck up the courage to open that door and go in uninvited. Then he knew. Ridiculous as it might appear, he was in love. Overcome with desire as he was, he knew that he must woo her, leading up to his declaration of love, hoping then to hear her admit, '*Moi, aussi, mon amour. je t'aime.*' Then, but not till then, could he take her in his arms, knowing that she was truly his, body and soul.

. . . . .

Christmas was upon them before they were hardly aware of it; the two of them intermingling their preparations with 'In England, we . . .' '. . . *Ah, oui, Monsieur*, but in France . . .' so that the house took on a gay, cosmopolitan look.

Edward had already received several invitations for the

46

Christmas season which he regretted he must decline unless it was possible to include a lady friend. It amused him to imagine their raised eyebrows; to hear their clacking tongues, but the hostesses, rather than lose the privilege of entertaining royalty, added the necessary invitation.

Thérèse-Bernadine was puzzled. She just could not understand the Prince's attitude, for while he showed every consideration towards her, he displayed no desire to share her bed. At times she felt piqued but then she would shrug her shoulders, telling herself she was once again living in luxury, why quarrel with her fate?

They had already slipped into a daily routine, Edward rising early and not seeing her until lunch-time. They never lingered over the meal for the Prince always had a vast amount of office work requiring his attention, while she, having an aptitude for making her own gowns, was never idle or bored.

When, however, in the romantic setting of candle-light and gleaming silver, they met for dinner, the atmosphere was vibrant and expectant. Each was playing a part; she taking such fastidious care with her toilette and choice of gown hoping to pierce the armour of this strange man while he was all charm and tenderness, striving to win her love.

When he discovered she was a good listener, conversation became much easier, he taking a great delight in regaling her with stories of his unhappy childhood; his equally miserable years as a military cadet and finally his painful affair with Adelaide. It was as though, by the telling, he unburdened himself, paving the way to a new freedom on which to base a new life with Thérèse-Bernadine.

·   ·   ·   ·   ·

They spent Christmas Eve round the harpsichord, learning each other's national carols, their voices raised in jubilation and laughter, until, nearing midnight, Thérèse excused

47

herself, reminding Edward that he had given her permission to attend Midnight Mass. At first, he had been reluctant that she should go. '. . . but so late! The streets will be full of drunken soldiers and their women . . .'

'I shall be perfectly safe, Sir. The Virgin and the Holy Child will protect me . . .'

'You must take the carriage . . . and Beck shall accompany you.'

Yet when she slipped noiselessly down the stairs, it was to find Edward, not Beck, awaiting her.

'I decided, Madame, though not a Catholic, I would like to accompany you.'

'You are indeed welcome, Sir.'

They barely spoke as they drove along. The church was crowded but in the dim light of the candles, Edward had little fear of being recognised. The reverence of the worshippers, the intoning of the priests and the hushed atmosphere of sanctity, culminating in the blessing of the crib, moved him deeply.

As they came out they were caught up in the press of people and to prevent them from being parted, Edward put a firm protective arm around Thérèse, shielding her as they walked across to the waiting carriage. Then as they swayed and jolted along the cobbled roadway, he found he had taken her hand between his.

She looked up and spoke tremulously, '*Joyeux Noel, Monsieur.*'

'A Happy Christmas, Madame,' and in that moment all barriers went crashing. She was in his arms and their lips met in their first kiss. He could not let her go, kissing her eyes and throat, murmuring huskily, 'I love you. I love you. Thérèse-Bernadine, I love you.'

'*Et moi aussi,*' came back the whisper. '*Je t'aime, mon prince.*'

She had said it. This woman, a jewel, priceless above all jewels, was his.

48

They came down to earth as they breakfasted together the next morning.

'Thérèse-Bernadine, I cannot continue to call you Madame. Neither can I spare the time to address you by your long name when I have so many other things I wish to say to you. Have you no other name?'

She grinned roguishly. 'Having given me my important sounding name, Papa quickly discovered the same trouble ... so ... to him, I became "Julie"!'

'The very name for you! Julie. My own beautiful little Julie.' He went silent for a moment. 'I have but one regret, *ma perle* . . . that I cannot make you my lawful wife.'

'Do not dwell on it, Sir. I know only too well the impossibility . . .'

'But I swear to you, *ma mignonne*, that in the eyes of God, I regard you as my true, loving wife, not just for now, but for all time . . .'

She put her fingers across his lips. 'Do not tempt fate, Sir. I am happy to live for the day . . .'

'No, *ma perle*, no. I see our lives ahead . . . always together . . .' She silenced him with a kiss, bringing fierce retaliation from Edward, holding her close as though never to let her go.

      .   .   .   .   .

General O'Hara and Colonel Symes were feeling decidedly uneasy and embarrassed. They had had to bow to Edward's ultimatum and entertain the French lady or spoil the garrison's Christmas festivities. Admittedly the society of Gibraltar was notoriously promiscuous . . . but that His Highness should so openly flout the conventions! They decided to wait until the New Year and then speak their minds . . . in the Prince's own interests of course. Perhaps he would dispense with the lady's services ere long, recalling that his affair with Mlle. Dubos had not been of long duration.

There was much speculation as to the conduct and out-come of Edward's first dinner-party, but all went away, ladies and gentlemen alike, declaring that His Highness had indeed excellent taste . . . and not only in food and wine! Julie had proved herself the perfect hostess, welcoming Edward's guests with charm and dignity, then gracefully circulating to ensure everyone's ease and pleasure. Never-theless, with Colonel Symes under strict orders to send detailed reports as to the Prince's conduct, the situation could not be tolerated.

It was with great diffidence that he approached Edward, his opening gambit being to congratulate him on the success-ful assembly. 'The lady, Sir. Will she be staying on the Rock any length of time?'

Edward stared haughtily at his mentor. 'I do not see, Sir, that the lady's movements are any concern of yours.'

'Your pardon, Sir, but I beg to differ. As you are well aware, I have to acquaint His Majesty . . .'

'. . . That I am living with a lady. I shall not contradict you, Sir.'

'But Your Highness, why evoke more censure? Sooner or later, you and the lady will go your separate ways . . . why not sooner . . . ?'

'Be so good, Sir, as to make yourself more explicit.' There was a rising indignation in Edward's voice.

'Very well, Sir. 'Tis notorious that these ladies are always willing to accept a present . . . a parting gift by way of recompense for losing their comfortable living. Say . . . two hundred pounds . . . or perhaps in your case, three hundred . . .'

'How dare you!' Indignation had now been superseded by fury. 'You over-step yourself, Sir. The lady is not for sale! Send your report and be damned! Embroider it with as many exaggerations as you wish . . . it will make no difference as far as I am concerned.'

Colonel Symes realised the futility of further argument.

Until now, both he and General O'Hara had been tactful in their reports, glossing over Edward's harshness, as having beneficial results, for every letter that left the Rock, whether from high-ranking officer or humble serving soldier, told the same story of undue severity and brutal treatment. Perhaps those complaints might now receive some attention.

.   .   .   .   .

It was incredible. Unbelievable. He had been ordered to proceed to Canada still in command of the Fusiliers. Why? Why not home to England to receive his dukedom? Why across the vast Atlantic to the icy, open space of North America, with civilisation only in its infancy? Only too well, he knew that it was because of his refusal to dismiss Julie. Would she be prepared to accompany him?

General O'Hara and his satellites rejoiced they were being relieved of their embarrassments, but the morale of the troops sank to a lower level of misery. What would happen to them, away across the sea where their miseries would go unheeded; where His Royal Highness could wield the whip with none to hear their screams but wild animals, but they surely no more savage than their bestial colonel? They spat each time his name was mentioned. How many of them would ever see England again?

.   .   .   .   .

Julie was quick to sense Edward's distress. 'Perhaps, Sir, if I was to return to France or Spain . . . it might ease the situation. You could be allowed to remain here . . . or return to England . . .'

'Julie . . . Julie . . . I could not contemplate life without you . . . neither in England nor here . . . nor anywhere else in the world. Do you . . . do you wish to leave me?'

51

She was in his arms immediately. 'Indeed, no. Oh never, but for your sake there is nothing I would not do . . .'

'Would you accompany me to Canada . . . not knowing the living conditions . . .'

'Willingly, Edward, willingly. So long as you want me, I will never leave you . . .'

'Then it is settled, *ma perle.*' He held her close. 'Thank God for your love, Julie. It is the only worth-while thing in my life. Perhaps we shall find an unexpected happiness in the new country. Who knows?'

.   .   .   .   .

Despite his optimism, Edward occasionally had fits of deep depression mainly concerned with what he considered his unfair treatment. Then he would shut himself up in his office until the mood passed, giving orders that he was not to be disturbed; that he was 'out' to all callers, so that when a gentle tap on the door roused him from his melancholy, he inwardly swore fiercely. 'Blast the man!' Typical of the discipline. Forgetful of orders, but when the discreet tap was repeated, he violently bade to enter.

His batman, recruited from the Queen's, looked crestfallen as Edward glared at him.

'Sir. The gentleman refused to leave . . . said he would wait until you . . .'

'His name, dolt? Did you not ask his name?'

'He refused to give it. Said he wished to surprise Your Highness. He . . . he is an officer in His Majesty's Navy . . .'

Edward's shout of jubilation as he jumped from his chair caused the batman to regard him with some alarm. Dashing across the hallway, he unceremoniously flung open the library door and then paused as a short stocky figure turned from the window but only for a second as both men moved forward to meet in a close embrace.

'William!'

'Edward.' For a moment they remained with their arms around each other, then simultaneously drew apart, their faces alight with regard and affection.

'God! What a height you've grown, Edward! When I last saw you . . .'

'That was seven years ago, brother.' He held out a glass of wine. 'I think you'll find this to your liking, William. The port and Madeira that we get here are about our only luxuries. To your health, brother, and our happy meeting.'

There was a merry twinkle in William's blue, protruding eyes. '. . . and to the ladies, Edward, bless 'em. Never forget the ladies, Edward.'

The clink of glasses rang across the room as the brothers seated themselves, William tasting the wine with an air of a connoisseur.

'Yes. 'Tis good. Rich and full of flavour.'

'I drink but little myself . . .'

'Still the Simon Pure, eh? Come now, Edward, women and wine provide the mainspring of life, but then, as regards the women, Simon Pure has defected, has he not?'

'Then you know?'

'Of a surety, but George and Fred are all sympathy, while I, who adore all ladies, have purposely called in the hope of meeting the lady before you transport her across the ocean —and to ask a favour.'

Edward ignored his brother's bantering tone, seemingly lost in his thoughts. 'You don't understand, William. You . . . and George . . . and Fred . . . and my younger brothers have your affairs and beyond a certain amount of mild criticism, little obstruction is put in your way. You have been given your dukedom. Fred received his when he was twenty-one. I am now twenty-three without either dukedom or adequate allowance for my rank.'

'I know, dear boy. I know.'

'I was sent here because I had the audacity to return home without permission to plead my rights . . .' His voice

53

trailed away . . . 'but you know the outcome of that escapade. Now they would separate me from the woman I love.'

William looked up sharply, curiosity in his eyes. 'The real passion, Edward? You must tell me about her.'

'Julie? She is all I shall ever want in a woman. She has great beauty, charm and gaiety and gentleness. She is not only good to me but good for me, giving me that affection that has been denied me all my life. She is both my beloved and my mother . . .'

'Now, now, Edward, forget the maternal affection. Love between a man and a woman is a thing apart . . . something that no-one can define. Many times, I thought I had found the perfect love, but . . .' He shook his head in negation, then bending forward, he continued with a tone of conspiracy, '. . . but I'll tell you something, Edward, that as yet I have not discussed with either George or Fred. I too am convinced that I have met the real love of my life . . .'

'Then I am indeed happy for you, William. And the lady?'

'She is an actress at Drury Lane . . .'

'An actress!' There was dismay in Edward's voice, recalling actresses of his acquaintance.

'Yes, an actress, brother. You need not be so pompous. She is Mrs. Dorothy Jordan. So far, I have not declared myself but judging from her cordial manner when we have met, I feel sure she returns my affection. Wish me luck, Edward.'

'With all my heart,' but as he voiced the words, he doubted the outcome. William's affairs with the ladies were notorious. 'You mentioned a favour?'

'Ah, yes. A certain petty-officer, Mr. Robert Wood, until now my personal servant, is desirous of a passage to Quebec.' He laughed jovially. 'He too, poor fellow, has succumbed to Cupid's darts and is desirous to hasten across the sea to marry his love. Being a first-class sailor—and a trusty servant—he would be very useful in your household during the voyage.'

Edward smiled. 'I think that can easily be arranged. Now come, you must stay to dinner and meet my beloved Julie.'

·　　·　　·　　·　　·

Now that Edward's departure was so imminent, General O'Hara could not be too gushing or effusive, loudly extolling his good work. Such splendid service could not pass without worthy recognition.

On a lovely May evening, the Rock resounded and re-echoed with music from the Hôtel de l'Europe. General O'Hara was holding a farewell assembly in honour of Prince Edward's departure. The ballroom was a riot of colour; army officers preening themselves in their brilliant dress uniforms; naval officers, fortunate enough to be in the vicinity with their vessels, displaying a variety of many hued mess-jackets ablaze with decorations, while the ladies, all wearing new gowns specially bought for the occasion, vied one with the other as to who could display more jewels . . . and bosom.

Edward, as guest of honour, had been afforded a seat under a canopy of pink silk where he had to listen to a speech eulogising his virtues. He was glad he had Julie by his side. This he had insisted upon. It was not exactly a gesture of defiance but more to prove his esteem and regard for her. Let those who objected, stay away. No invitation had been refused. Now he knew he had been right for surely there was no other woman present who was her equal either in beauty or decorum.

For three hours they danced to the fifty-strong orchestra; a night to be remembered . . . to be remembered also by the serving-ranks who, as the strains of music reached them in their squalid quarters, felt their spirits sink lower and lower, wondering as to what lay ahead of them.

. . . . .

Yet despite all the good wishes and adulation, Edward's heart was heavy; not only that he was being sent to Canada instead of returning to England, but that he was leaving the Rock so heavily in debt. He still owed £20,000 in Geneva. Then he hit on what seemed to him a brilliant idea. He would issue bonds to this value to be repaid in five years' time with five per cent interest. To his delight, there was an immediate response, all the money forthcoming from the more wealthy citizens of the Rock, who appeared to forget that His Highness also owed them several thousands. To raise still more money, he decided to sell all his personal equipment, drawing mild criticism from Julie.

'But, Sir, think of the enormous expense to replace everything.'

'. . . there will be the money from the sale . . .'

'. . . it will fetch but little, Sir . . . and moreover in Quebec, will there be the same quality available?'

'I could have another equipment sent out from England . . .'

'At great expense, Sir, yes. But think of the time you would be without . . . while your order was going across the ocean; while the goods were being packed and despatched to you . . .'

He laughed good-naturedly, his spirits restored, 'Dear little Julie . . . so thrifty and wise. What would I do without you?'

. . . . .

It was towards the end of June before they set sail on the frigate *Resistance*. Following in their wake was the

Ulysses, its bulwarks strained to capacity with the unhappy men of Edward's regiment.

As they waved their last farewells, Edward was surprised to see tears coursing down Julie's cheeks.

'Why so sad, *ma mignonne*? Is it that you regret going so far away from home?'

She shook her head. 'No, Sir, no,' she whispered. 'Just . . . just that I feel I owe so much to Gibraltar . . . for it was here . . . it was the Rock that brought us together.'

He put a comforting arm around her and raised her hand to his lips. 'I too shall always be grateful . . . remembering every Christmas morning the awakening of our love. Come, *ma petite*, let us go below and see what miracles Philip Beck and Robert Wood have performed by way of making our cabins more comfortable.'

3

It would seem that all Quebec was waiting at the quay-side to welcome His Royal Highness, Prince Edward. Two years ago, they had entertained Prince William for a brief period while his ship lay off Quebec, but now, this military brother was to be stationed here indefinitely. On a raised dais, roped off from the surging, pushing crowd, stood the Governor of Quebec, Lord Dorchester, accompanied by his wife. It was a motley crowd; soldiers in scarlet uniforms; French priests in sombre black; trappers wearing fur hats with the animal's tail still attached; Indians, some with their faces painted and clutching tomahawks, giving cause to the more sober citizens, business men and farmers to put protective arms around their women and children.

Suddenly a cry went up. A vessel had rounded Port Levis. Then another, and as they watched, the *Resistance* and the *Ulysses* were sailing gently into the harbour. Now the ships broke flags and the breeze carried inland the loud vociferous cheers of the troops about to be liberated after being cooped up for seven weeks. Barren might be their new abode but at least they would have freedom to move; something to see more spectacular than water and sky.

Their cheering was answered by the striking up of the quay-side band and the sight of myriads of streamers fluttering down from the windows of buildings enclosing the harbour.

Edward was the first ashore to be greeted by a loyal speech from Lord Dorchester. It was obvious the reception touched him for as he replied, his voice was full of emotion. 'Sir, I request you will be fully convinced how grateful I must feel for the flattering sentiments you have expressed towards my person. I am anxious that during my stay in this country my conduct may prove I am deserving of them. Nothing will give me greater pleasure than if I shall be fortunate enough to find an opportunity of being personally serviceable to you. Till then I hope you will remain fully persuaded of my gratitude and esteem.'

In the background, Julie listened and watched with interest. How elegant were the ladies around the dais but how out-moded were their gowns! Still, it was a far cry from Paris, and Quebec was bound to be tardy in receiving the latest styles.

Along with the officers' wives, she had been shepherded to a reserved space where they could watch the proceedings prior to being driven off to their hotels.

As the civic and church dignitaries were being presented, the troops were being rapidly brought ashore to line up in serried ranks on the quay-side. When the last man was in position, there was a sudden roll of drums, which when it died away, left a silence only broken by the screeching of sea-gulls wheeling overhead. She saw the band-conductor raise his baton and then the strains of 'God Save the King' filled the air. Though a Frenchwoman, she felt a surge of loyalty towards the English throne. With another roll of drums, the regimental band gave warning that their colonel had taken up his position at the head of his regiment and was ready to march. Then to the sound of bugles and drums and clashing cymbals, they were away, legs and arms swinging in meticulous rhythm. Julie was entranced. Hitherto, she had seen little of Edward's prowess as a soldier.

Philip Beck, never far away, was ushering her towards a carriage, to follow the troops to a castle where a tremendous crowd awaited them, and there she watched with fascination as Lord Dorchester reviewed the regiment with Edward shouting commands. She was proud of him. How tall and handsome he was in his scarlet uniform gleaming with gilt buttons and tassels, offset by the tight, white knee-breeches and sword-belt. As for the black fur-cap with its large, white hackle-plume, she was always threatening to purloin one and start a new mode. Perhaps, out here in Quebec, she would do so. She was going to need a fur hat in Winter!

Once again, they were on the march, this time to Rue St. Louis, to Kent House where she and Edward were to live; there to deposit their flags before marching to the barracks.

During the long, weary weeks at sea, she and Edward had employed much time discussing their future. They were only too well aware that the people would guess and gossip as to their true state but past experience had taught them that none dare question. Let them believe what they wished—that they were married if gossip said so—but obviously she could not continue under the name of Mlle. de Mongenet. They would be living near the St. Lawrence river. Why not Madame de St. Lawrence? Or Laurent? By the time they reached Quebec, it had been settled. She was Madame Julie de St. Laurent.

They had also discussed their code of behaviour. Lady Dorchester, as ruler of Quebec society, was the terror of every young girl making her social début. Let her rise too quickly from her curtsey or move too quickly from a presence and Her Ladyship was quick to pounce. Fortunately, Edward had been told, the Dorchesters were shortly leaving for England, only staying to welcome him and present the leading personalities. Therefore to avoid the hazard of any friction, they decided Julie should remain in the background until after Her Ladyship's departure.

'I can assure you, my darling, that if she gives an assembly—which I expect she will—at which I shall be expected to dance with every lady she presents to me—I shall make use of those ladies to our advantage.'

Julie was puzzled. 'To our advantage, Sir? I do not understand.'

'Can you not hear them, *ma mignonne*? They will all be giving assemblies—all anxious to get me into their houses. I shall smile and accept their invitations, provided the charming Madame de St. Laurent is also invited.'

'You schemer, Edward!'

'At the same time, I shall be able to discern those ladies capable of being your good friends.'

So during the next few days, while Edward attended assemblies, balls and carnivals, some in honour of his arrival, others in honour of the Dorchesters' departure, Julie, aided by Philip Beck, put their new home in order, utilising furniture brought from Gibraltar, and visiting the stores to buy more. She had no fear of any lady enticing her prince.

.   .   .   .   .

Now that the troops were settled in, Edward was again insisting on early morning parades, his policy being, '*I have had to do, to suffer, to endure these things, What I have done, others can and shall do.*'

His domestic routine was still the same, lunch being the first break he allowed himself in a day's work, eating a hearty meal and then indulging in an hour's rest before resuming his paper work. This hour he now spent with Julie, both treating it as sacrosanct, Julie also making it known that she was never 'at home' until three o'clock.

It was therefore with a feeling of annoyance that they heard the knock on the door but when the footman announced that Mr. Robert Wood wished to see His Highness, Edward was quickly out of his chair, hand outstretched to greet him.

'Mr. Wood! This is a surprise. Madame, you remember Mr. Wood, do you not?'

'Indeed I do. How can I ever forget his services aboard the *Resistance*?'

Mr. Wood bowed graciously. 'I came to seek your aid, Sir.'

'Ah. Are you now married?'

'Not as yet, Sir. My prospective father-in-law only gave his consent provided I left the navy and joined him in his souvenir shop . . .'

'Well?'

'I find working for him very restricting. There are days when not a single customer crosses the threshold . . .'

'What you are saying, Mr. Wood, is that you would prefer a more manly job?'

'Exactly, Sir. Then I could marry . . .'

'Say no more. I will see to it.' He hesitated. 'There is a slight office you could perform for me.'

'With pleasure, Sir.'

'You will be delighted to learn that Madame and I were married in Malta before we sailed.'

'Congratulations, Sir . . . and Madame.'

Julie felt a wave of shame. Why need Edward lie? It was not in keeping with his character.

'. . . I would therefore appreciate it, if you could let this be discreetly known. As you know, Madame cannot take my name, so now she is known as Madame de St. Laurent.'

·   ·   ·   ·   ·

Both he and Julie were amazed at the rapid growth of their welcome. Everyone of any social standing was anxious to invite them into their home. To their satisfaction they discovered that it was not just because of Edward's royal rank for the majority of the Quebec folk chose to ignore all royal protocol. True, the ladies still made their curtsies, and the gentlemen's bows were as courteous as ever and Edward's arrival was always announced by a fanfare of trumpets, but after that, conversation and movement were free and easy. The ordinary folk had taken a liking to him, enjoying seeing a prince walking their streets without any airs or graces.

Among the first to give an assembly, inviting Edward and Julie as their guests of honour, were a certain Monsieur and Madame de Salaberry. Edward had already met them, taking an immediate liking to both, discovering that Louis de Salaberry belonged to a military family of many generations. He could sense from the moment he presented Julie, that there was instant rapport between them. For a while they conversed with the usual introductory pleasantries till Edward led Catherine de Salaberry on to the floor.

Louis de Salaberry was quick to apologise to Julie. 'I crave your pardon, Madame, that I cannot ask you to dance.' He patted his leg significantly, 'C'est la guerre,' he laughed.

'Then let us sit and watch the others spend their energy. I shall enjoy talking to a Frenchman. Have you lived in Canada long, Sir?'

'I was born here. My family came to Canada in 1665.'

'But you speak . . . you have the air as if you are accustomed to the Parisian salon.'

He laughed again. 'Despite my father accepting defeat at the hands of the British and transferring his allegiance, he sent me to France to be educated.'

'Then how come you to be so grievously wounded?'

'After my return to Canada, I soon grew tired of lounging around my father's estate, so when the Americans invaded Canada, I volunteered to join the English army.'

'Then England is much in your debt, Sir.'

Edward and Madame de Salaberry were now back but being an assiduous hostess, she was quickly presenting

Julie to another gentleman and finding another partner for Edward.

Driving home that night, Edward's arm around her as her head rested sleepily on his shoulder, she murmured, 'Louis de Salaberry. I found him most engaging.'

'. . . and I found his wife truly enchanting.'

'He told me of his service in the English army . . .'

'. . . and Madame told me that they have five children . . .'

They laughed together and kissed. 'We must invite them to dinner, *ma petite*; a private dinner, just the four of us. I should enjoy more conversation with the gentleman and Madame, I am sure, would be a most desirable companion for you.'

Perhaps it was because the de Salaberrys were Catholics that acted as a magnet drawing Julie into their family circle but within a very short time a rare, strong friendship had been cemented. With Edward, it was a totally different reason. For the first time in his life, he was experiencing the joy of true family life. The de Salaberry children romped and played with Papa and Mama; were very rarely chastised and stood neither in awe of them nor any of their distinguished visitors. When they came into a room, they did not bow and curtsey but made a concerted rush for their parents, to be kissed and cuddled and tossed into the air. When they misbehaved, they were scolded and punished but there were no beatings.

.   .   .   .   .

The de Salaberrys lived in a large rambling house at Beauport, a few miles out of Quebec, and as their visits became more frequent, Julie and Edward began to feel an urge to live in the country . . . to have a garden and grounds . . . and privacy.

'Wait until the Spring, Sir,' advised Louis. 'As yet, you have not experienced a Canadian winter.'

'Perhaps if you will then acquaint us as to any suitable property . . .'

'Indeed, Sir, I will make enquiries . . .'

'. . . not too far from Beauport,' interrupted Julie.

'Do not pester yourself, dear Julie. I shall take it upon myself to observe that point,' admonished Catherine laughingly. 'In the meantime don't forget you are coming to spend Christmas here with us.'

Christmas. Their first anniversary. Much as they still enjoyed being alone in each other's company, they realised that Christmas with the de Salaberrys would be joyous, happy and harmonious. He would be glad to take a few days' leave and get away from the barrack square, for here in Quebec new difficulties were presenting themselves. Drunkenness was always rife among the troops but since the advent of Winter, the men had turned to drinking rum in an endeavour to defeat the cold, especially when they were going on guard duty. Consequently, there had been many cases of drunken sentries . . . a crime which merited severe flogging. Edward was well aware of the mutterings and dissatisfaction; dissatisfaction that was being emphasised by the increased number of desertions.

Before his arrival it had been a common-place crime and his predecessors had laid down the punishment; 999 lashes and in some cases the death penalty. The government paid a reward of eight dollars for all recaptured deserters, with an additional eight dollars from the officers of the delinquent's regiment. Edward was untiring in his efforts to recapture every fusilier who dared to make the attempt, sadistically ordering the maximum penalty.

.   .   .   .   .   .

Catherine de Salaberry, watching her children's activities, beamed happily and at the first opportunity of speaking to Julie alone, whispered, 'Apart from Louis, you are the first to hear my news. I am going to have another baby. Next June.'

Julie hugged her friend. 'How wonderful! I'm so happy for you. I too want children. Not just yet; I'm selfish . . . I want Edward to myself a little longer. As you can see, he adores children, so that once he becomes a father . . . he will have little time for me.'

'No, Julie, no. It doesn't happen like that. As the mother of his children, you'll become dearer to him.'

The festivities over, they reluctantly bade their friends farewell, until they met at Julie's assembly on New Year's Eve.

Though it was bitterly cold, the sun was shining and with Edward at the reins, the cariole sped swiftly over the frozen road. Julie, well wrapped in furs, was bubbling over with high spirits, bursting to tell Edward the news.

'Madame de Salaberry confided in me the most wonderful piece of news,' she began.

Edward, watching the road, murmured something inaudible.

'. . . she is having another baby in June.'

'The devil she is! Five not sufficient?'

'Apparently not. Oh, I am so happy for her. *Une petite bébé!* Already, I'm longing to hold it . . .'

'Tell you what, Julie, we will offer to be its god-parents.' There was excitement in Edward's voice. 'If it is a boy, he shall be called Edward . . . and I'll enter him for the English army . . .'

'And if it is a girl?'

'She shall be called Julie.'

A silence fell between them. What a wonderful father he would make. How much longer would it be, before she had a wonderful secret to tell? She heard herself speaking her thoughts aloud.

'Would it not be wonderful, Edward, to have a family like the de Salaberrys?'

She was amazed at his reaction. First an uncanny silence, as though he was bereft of words, then harsh, violent denunciation.

'Never, Julie, never. There must be no children.'

Now it was her turn to be nonplussed, unable to believe her ears. 'But, Edward, surely you do not mean . . . you cannot mean . . . suppose we did have a child.'

'It would have to be sent away . . . fostered out . . .'

She jerked at the reins in his hands, then pulled hard, so that the horses slowed down and stopped.

They faced each other, he cold and hard; she flushed with anger.

'Why? Other princes do not deny their natural children.'

'No? Have you ever heard of my brother the Prince of Wales and Mrs. Fitzherbert playing the happy parents?'

'Has she . . . has there been a child?'

'Who knows? George told me that he and Maria have a definite understanding. Any child . . . discreetly placed . . .'

'And you would have it that way with us?'

'I would. I could not bear the ignominy of the common herd discussing my bastard parentage . . . the jokes . . . the lampoons . . .'

'But . . . but you are fond of children. You idolise the young de Salaberrys . . .'

'They happen to be legally and lawfully begotten . . .'

'How dare you! You insult me, Sir!'

'Julie . . . Julie . . . What are we saying to each other? The occasion has not arisen.'

She did not answer and the rest of the journey was completed in silence but that night she bolted her door against him; not so much to bar his entry but to give her the freedom to weep.

. . . . . .

For several days they hardly spoke to each other but with

the approach of the New Year's Eve assembly, she knew she must make the peace for never would she let him down; she must be the perfect hostess . . . a happy, smiling, perfectly-at-ease hostess. During their hour after lunch, she brought down the gown she had just completed, a pink polonaise over a lace petticoat. She held it before her. 'Do you like it, Sir?'

For answer, he rose and crushed her in his arms, regardless of the gown.

'Julie . . . Julie . . .' His voice was broken with emotion. 'I thought I'd lost you for ever.' He took her in his arms holding her close, then kissing her tenderly, releasing her, holding her at arms' length, to inspect the dress . . . 'Beautiful . . . but never so beautiful as my Julie.'

Back to their delightful intimacy, she tried to convince herself, if ever there was a baby, all would be well but she had to confide in Catherine, telling all that had passed between her and Edward.

Madame de Salaberry was amazed. 'C'est impossible. He adores children . . . he worships you . . .'

'Maybe . . . but not a bastard child . . .' She stopped abruptly remembering the de Salaberrys were unaware of their true state, another matter which Edward did not wish to be discussed.

'Any marriage between us would be morganatic,' she faltered. 'The children would be of no consequence . . . they could not inherit any title . . . but even so, we could make them happy . . .'

Catherine put a comforting arm around her, 'If you were to have a child, he would want the babe as much as you . . .'

'That is what I keep telling myself but I am not so sure. Edward's pride is his big stumbling block . . . Oh, how I envy you, dear Souris, of the little one in June.'

* * * * *

68

They found their ideal country retreat, Montmorency House about six miles out of Quebec. It was a large wooden house with extensive grounds within sight and sound of a swift tumbling waterfall that poured into the St. Lawrence river. Now that they were near neighbours of the de Salaberrys, hardly a day went by when the friends did not meet; Edward calling as he passed to and from the barracks, while Julie would never have dreamt of driving into Quebec without dropping in on dear Souris, as she was known to her more intimate friends.

When the news was brought that Souris had given birth to a baby boy, she was almost as overjoyed as if the child had been her own and immediately wrote her congratulations.

'Hurrah! Hurrah! Hurrah! A thousand rounds in honour of the charming Souris and the new born. In truth my head is full of joy and my hand trembles so much that I can scarcely hold my pen. And it is another boy! How I wish that I was one of those powerful fairies who were able to bestow their gifts in such profusion; how the dear child should be endowed. Unfortunately all this is but an illusion, but never mind, something has said to me that the pretty little fellow has been born under a happy star; kiss him for me, my dear friend, and tell him the prediction of his god-mother. Oh! No! I was never so happy in my life . . . I will come to Beauport today about seven o'clock; tomorrow I will go again and every day. Ah! I wish it could be this very instant of my life. I reserve it to myself to congratulate Madame de Salaberry in person on the happy event; in the meantime, I embrace the whole household without distinction of age or sex.'

If she was to be denied the joy of motherhood, she was going to make the most of being a god-mother.

The christening preparations began with rather a delicate

problem. Edward was a Protestant and in the eyes of the Catholic clergy, a heretic, therefore not suitable as a god-father, but upon Edward's insistence the difficulties were overcome or rather by-passed and the boy was named Edward, the actual ceremony being a most brilliant affair with a detachment of Royal Fusiliers being in attendance.

During the Autumn months, they travelled as far as Lake Ontario, visiting Fort Niagara where a ball was held in their honour with Mohawks in war paint and feathers per-forming their war dance. It was all very exciting and col-ourful but Julie much preferred the company of her dear de Salaberrys.

. . . . .

It was most disturbing that only a few days before Christmas, Captain Wetherall, one of the gentlemen attached to his household, should inform him of rumours of mutiny.

He liked Frederick Wetherall; young, trustworthy and a true soldier. He would not imagine or exaggerate mere gossip.

'The plot, Sir, is that the men should break out of barracks during the night, come here to Kent House, murder you and then burn down the house.'

'And then what will they do?' asked Edward mildly.

'Their idea is to get across the river, or failing that, to sell their lives as dearly as possible.'

Edward paced the room thoughtfully, then, 'I do not think they have the guts to do it. What is your opinion, Sir?'

'My information was given by one who is desirous for your safety. He had heard it from a drunken soldier . . . unknown to him, but obviously one of the conspirators.'

'Make enquiries, Wetherall. In the meantime, do not go abroad without a pistol. Pass this order to all other officers. Order more barrack inspections. Double the sentry guards.'

He must do something to appease the men. Mutiny was the last thing he wanted. Back in England, it would spell failure.

The next morning, he addressed the troops lined up on the barrack square. Without any quibbling, he told them that he had heard rumours of an intended mutiny. What were their grievances? Too severe punishment? Only miscreants, defaulters and trouble-makers were punished.

It was nearing Christmas time however, and he was prepared to make concessions and to listen to their complaints.

He was surprised at all the trifling items to which they objected, but promised to rectify most of them. The principal complaint, however, stressed their bitterness at the brief liberty they were allowed. Only two hours each night. Here, Edward was adamant. Two hours was long enough to go drinking rum and brawling with each other and innocent citizens of Quebec.

. . . .

He had been thankful to go to Beauport to relax and enjoy the company of his friends. Before they left Quebec, the Christmas mails had arrived bringing him the heart-warming news that his father was prepared to pay his Gibraltar debts. Did this mean that his father was beginning to have more regard for him?

There was a letter from William telling him that he had now set up an establishment with Mrs. Jordan and that they were both deliriously happy. Their brother Frederick Duke of York had married Princess Frederica of Prussia and they too appeared to be happy. Fervently, Edward hoped that for the ladies' sakes his brothers would now mend their ways.

Julie too had had letters from her family; letters which made little mention of the Revolution but Julie could read the fear between the lines. Often were the times when she found herself wondering as to the safety of Jean de Fortisson and the Marquis de Permangle.

Despite Edward's good news about his debts she could sense that something was bothering him but she had long since learned never to question him. Yet once in the company of the children, she was glad to see all traces of perplexity disappear.

.   .   .   .   .

The New Year was but two days old and Private Draper was drunk again; too drunk to go on sentry duty. Seeking a replacement and finding none willing, he became abusive. Abuse was answered by abuse and when an officer came on the scene, the whole plot came tumbling out and six ring-leaders were under arrest.

The news was conveyed to Edward immediately. He gave a sigh of relief that the danger had passed; that the mutiny had been bloodless, not one shot having been fired.

The court-martial began the following week. Edward was amazed at the vindictiveness of the ring-leaders, one of them turning King's evidence.

The plot had been to persuade the whole regiment to mutiny; those who were unwilling were to be shot. The Prince was to be taken prisoner and Kent House set on fire. Private Rose, another ring-leader, was then to demand of the Prince, redress for their complaints and a free pardon for all the mutineers. If the Prince refused, he was to be killed together with all the other officers, except for any prepared to join them.

The court-martial lasted a fortnight, the sentences being death for Private Draper, 700 lashes for Private Kennedy, 400 lashes for Sergeant Wigton—and reduced to private—300 lashes for Private Rose. Those sentenced to flogging were to be sent home to England to await His Majesty's pleasure, which they knew would be transportation for life.

Now that Edward was able to tell of his fears over Christmas and the New Year, Julie was all contrition that she had failed to understand his mood. She shivered with horror whenever she thought of what might have happened to her beloved Edward.

* * * * *

As she drove to Beauport, the leisurely clip-clop of the horse drawing the cariole was, save for the singing of birds, the only sound to disturb the April morning. She was out early for Edward had not come home last night. With this horrible execution business hanging over Quebec she had not expected him. Thank goodness it would soon be ended. Of course, Private Draper, when he led that futile attempt on Edward's life, must have known that he would face the death penalty. Yet her tender heart was deeply moved as it had been when she heard of the vicious floggings the other culprits had suffered. For that reason, she was seeking the company of Catherine de Salaberry, the only person to whom she could speak freely.

Catherine greeted her warmly. The children came running in, and there were kisses and hugs from them all, but Madame de Salaberry, discerning Julie's distress beneath the bright façade, suggested they should pay a visit to the silk mercers, for both ladies fashioned many of their own gowns.

As they drove along, they found conversation difficult, each knowing what was uppermost in the other's thoughts. Mercifully by now, military law would have exacted its price for treason.

The streets seemed unusually deserted for this hour of the morning. Hearing in the not-too-far-off distance the strains of a military band, Julie drew in the reins. They listened attentively. Strange music . . . funereal . . . a funeral march. Slowly she drove along to where the street merged with the main thoroughfare, now lined with rows and rows of people.

'Let us go back,' urged Catherine, 'and take another way . . .'

'No. I want to see what it is about.' Her voice was dull and toneless.

The music was coming nearer. Then from the driving seat, they saw Edward, tall and regal, conspicuous in full dress uniform, leading the strangest procession Quebec had ever seen. Behind him, in slow march, came a detachment of Fusiliers under arms. She involuntarily drew her breath as a gun-carriage came round the bend, bearing a black coffin, but the next moment a strangled cry escaped her, as she stared unbelievingly at the pitiable semblance of a man, ashen-faced, stumbling along, dressed in a shroud. To complete the hideousness, the regimental band brought up the rear, playing more sombre dirges.

Catherine had hidden her face in her hands, but Julie, as though mesmerised, watched until the procession was out of sight.

'I thought the execution was early this morning,' she whispered, then finding strength in her voice, 'How could he? Oh, how could he?'

Catherine de Salaberry placed a comforting arm around her. 'It is not for us to reproach, Julie . . .'

'But the cruelty! Is it not enough that the man has to die?'

'His Highness is not the first to devise such a macabre warning to would-be defaulters. Governor Simcoe had a deserter shot while kneeling on his coffin . . .'

'Oh stop, Catherine, stop. I can bear no more . . .'

•   •   •   •   •   •

Edward came home early in the afternoon. She was in her room, and when she heard his quick step on the stairs, she was thankful she had bolted the door. He seemed surprised when the door refused to open, rattling the knob violently, calling in a jovial, pleasant voice, 'Open the door Julie. It's Edward.'

'Go away. I never want to speak to you again.'

'Julie. What game is this? Open the door.'

'I saw you this morning,' she shouted back. 'Saw you at the head of that horrible procession . . .'

'Oh, that. Open the door, Julie, and I'll tell you all about it . . .'

'I don't want to know. I saw too much.'

The argument continued for some time, until Edward, becoming angry, hurled himself downstairs into his cariole and drove back to Quebec.

When Catherine called the next day, she found Julie quite composed. '*Ah, ma chérie*, naturally you are now much relieved since His Highness has explained.'

'Explained?'

'About Private Draper. His reprieve at the last moment.'

'No. What happened?'

'Well, Monsieur de Salaberry was present as a spectator and saw what happened. Private Draper was tied to the stake and the firing squad took up its position. Then His Royal Highness went up to speak to the condemned man. Read him a lecture about his evil ways and the hope that he had learned his lesson, but that now, he, Prince Edward, had forgiven him, he was a free man. Then the procession re-formed and they returned to Quebec. Was it not magnanimous of the Prince?'

'Magnanimous? To cause all that mental suffering? It was bestial, sadistic . . . abhorrent . . .'

'Listen to me, Julie. A soldier lives two separate lives. I should know. My father was a soldier. I married a soldier. When he buckles on his sword, he becomes another being, far removed from the man who the night before held you in his arms . . . Now come back to Beauport with me and stay for dinner. I will send a message into Quebec, asking His Hignness to join us.'

'Oh, Souris, dear Souris, thank you so much. I've been almost out of my mind wondering how I could make the peace. I sent him away yesterday afternoon . . . and he has not yet returned.'

For a moment Catherine was silent, then gently, 'Be advised, Julie, avoid such tactics.'

There was something in her voice that caused Julie to speak sharply. 'So you have heard the rumours? . . . But it's not true . . . vile, evil gossip. Just because occasionally . . . when staying in Quebec, His Highness has visited the house opposite . . . Just because Miss Eliza Green is staying there with her sister . . .'

'Miss Eliza Green so happens to have a rather unenviable reputation . . . but dear Julie, like you, I am positive that it is nothing but wicked gossip.'

'The Prince would never be false to me . . .' There was pride in her voice, '. . . but oh, how relieved I shall be when he arrives at Beauport tonight.'

4

They had now been in Quebec for two years and Edward was beginning to feel restless and bored, anxious for a more active form of service. Occasional letters from his brothers told of the prowess of Ernest and Augustus on the battlefield; of their wounds and the adulation poured on them by their parents and sisters. Almost three years since that mad dash from Geneva! Surely his father should now relent and ask him to return home. Hopefully he wrote to the King suggesting that he should take his part in the war against France but there was no reply. All he could do to relieve the tedium was to undertake more explorations, but the heat of Autumn was so oppressive, the climate suiting neither him nor Julie, that they found it more beneficial to rest at Montmorency House.

Of course there was the continuous social round of Quebec with hostesses clamouring for their patronage but an over-saturation of balls and levées found Julie and Edward politely declining, preferring the peace of their library, for both were inveterate readers. Lord and Lady Dorchester were back from their trip to England and although Edward had perforce to attend all her assemblies, she still ignored Julie. Even at the November ball given in honour of Edward's birthday, Julie had to be content to be just one of the crowd, with Lady Dorchester beside Edward. Not that Julie held any rancour; she was quite happy as one of Catherine de Salaberry's party.

. . . . . .

It was cruel that the so long-awaited orders should arrive on Christmas Eve . . . their third anniversary . . . orders for Prince Edward, now promoted to the rank of Major-General, to proceed to the West Indies, there to fight the French.

The news at first overwhelmed him, and noting Julie's abject appearance, protested. '*This is more of my father's devilish machinations. The West Indies! The wish entertained about me in certain quarters when serving there is that I might fall,*' but surmounting the shock, he began to feel elated. He was going on active service!

Julie, however, could not hide her misery and fears at the thought of separation; at the prospect that Edward might be killed or maimed or taken prisoner or lost at sea.

When she voiced her fears, he laughed. 'Oh, no, *ma petite.* Rather do I see the prospect of going home. I shall acquit myself well, then my father must perforce ask me to return to England.'

'. . . and I . . .' she began tremulously.

'I have been giving the matter much thought. I think our best plan would be that you should go to England immediately upon my departure . . . there to await my arrival.'

'England! Are you so sure . . . that you will be going? That I will be allowed to . . . ?'

'To live as we now do? Rest assured, little Julie. I have no wish to live anywhere without you. You know London, do you not?'

She felt her colour rising remembering her visits in the company of Jean de Fortisson and Phillipe-Claude. 'Ye-e-e-s and I do have several friends . . . émigrés . . . now there.'

'Then that is settled. You go to England. It will be a pleasant way to spend the time of our separation. All being well, I shall join you in London. If I do not, I shall send for you to join me wherever I may be.'

'But how? It takes weeks for a letter . . . and the same for my return . . .'

'Before leaving, I intend to write to Mr. Coutts. I shall put you and all your affairs into his hands. He will keep you supplied with money . . . keep in touch with the War Office so that he knows my movements and can accordingly instruct you. Perfectly straightforward, *ma chérie*.'

Julie listened to his cool, pedantic voice with rising consternation. 'Could I not remain here, Sir? I have many friends . . .'

Edward sighed. 'But can you not see, *ma petite*, that I might sail direct for England from the West Indies. Then our period of separation would be lengthened.' Taking pity on her forlorn appearance, he compromised. 'Listen then, *ma mignonne*. You shall travel with me as far as Boston. I will arrange your passage from there.'

She knew it was no use arguing. Edward always had the last word. But what would happen if Edward was killed and she was stranded in London? . . . and the thought of leaving the de Salaberrys filled her with anguish.

Edward's spirits continued to rise. He would take Captain Wetherall as his aide-de-camp and Robert Wood should go as his personal servant. He had secured for him the post of door-keeper at the Legislative Assembly and although now married he knew he would welcome a taste of adventure.

It would be good, too, to get away from Miss Eliza Green and temptation. Thank God Julie knew nothing of the affair.

•　　•　　•　　•　　•　　•

It was indeed heart-breaking saying farewell to the de Salaberrys, but after many embraces and hugging of the children, and promises that they would write, Julie and Edward left Quebec at the end of January.

With the Winter at the height of its severity, with lakes and waterways being frozen over, Edward decided that the quickest and safest route for the first part of the journey would be overland. All went well, until crossing Lake Champlain, the ice gave way and the sled carrying Edward's personal equipment sank to the bottom. A fine beginning, he thought. Typical of the way Fate treated him. £2,000 worth of equipment gone to the fishes.

Expressing a wish that she should see New York, Edward was agreeable and after several days in Boston, where they were both most warmly welcomed and entertained, he saw her aboard the packet, but when the moment of parting came she could not hold back her tears, fully convinced that whether Edward lived or died, she would never see him again. 'Forgive me, Sir,' she whispered. 'I am a craven coward, but remember, dear love, that whatever happens, I shall always love you . . . and . . . thank you a million times for your love for me.'

He attempted to comfort her, holding her close, kissing and caressing her and then speaking of more practical matters. 'We shall meet, *ma perle*, either in London or Halifax. That . . . that is as sure as I now hold you in my arms. From New York, take a packet to Halifax. I have written Sir John Wentworth who will meet you and entertain you until you sail for England.'

She pouted, 'I have heard much against Lady Wentworth's mode of behaviour . . .'

He laughed, glad to relieve the tension. 'You ladies! Yes, Frances Wentworth has been quite a gay spark, but now as a middle-aged matron and mother, she is quite companionable.'

'Do not pester yourself, Sir. I, too, will be companionable.'

'How well I know it. Madame de St. Laurent never does or says the wrong thing. That is why I am so full of happy anticipation when I join you in London. And now, *ma perle*, I must go ashore.' He took her in his arms again, kissing her gently. '. . . and thank you too for your understanding love . . . and may the day come quickly for our reunion.'

As he went down the gangway, his elation rose to a still higher pitch. Soon . . . soon . . . he would be face to face with the enemy . . . actually in the line of fire.

.   .   .   .   .

Now that she was alone, save for her small household under the capable survey of Philip Beck, she decided to see as much of New York as possible but as soon as her identity and presence became known, certain papers took a delight in publishing scurrilous items about her and Edward, so taking the first packet available she set sail for Halifax.

Arriving there, she was dismayed to find that she could not obtain a passage to England for several weeks and had perforce to remain the guest of the Wentworths until on the 9th May, she bade them farewell from the deck of the *Portland*.

.   .   .   .   .

Edward, too, found that he had to wait longer for a ship than he had anticipated, but that gave him time to collect together another equipment . . . and to enjoy more entertainment.

It was early in March when he arrived at the island of Martinique, sweltering in tropical heat, waiting for General Sir Charles Grey to launch an attack on Fort Royal, the island's capital.

He was immediately given the command of two battalions. He was fanatically eager to get to grips with the enemy, full of the lust for war; to kill and maim, or be killed himself. He had a fatalistic notion of death. If he was to be killed in battle, what more noble end? Regardless of danger, he strode forward, leading his men into the city, brandishing his sword right and left while the troops with fixed bayonets followed his example, quickly routing the

French, sending them into hiding wherever they could find shelter. Ruthlessly, Edward ordered that they should be brought out at bayonet point, at the same time destroying all supplies of ammunition they came across. With the arrival of more British troops, the French commander surrendered to prevent further bloodshed. Martinique was in the hands of the British.

There were riotous celebrations in the officers' mess that night, with none more jubilant than Edward. His first military engagement had been successful! Sir Charles Grey had been most effusive in his congratulations, stating that he would most certainly be mentioning his courage and devotion to duty in the despatches home to England. Perhaps then his father might look more favourably upon him; perhaps order him home to England. There was nothing he desired more.

Despite the late night and drinking more than usual, he was up and about early the next morning for the British troops were helping the French to collect their dead and wounded. Edward, keeping a watchful eye on his men lest there should be any looting of the dead bodies, was horrified at the sight of the piled-up masses of corpses; some limbless; some headless, their uniforms dyed black with their own dried-up blood; bodies of brave men who had stood up against the English, barring the way into Fort Royal, and had forfeited their lives in doing so. This then was war stripped of its glory. How easily he could have been one of those already stinking, rotting corpses.

Yet, when next day orders came that they were embarking immediately for an attack on St. Lucia, he no longer felt any horror or revulsion.

Santa Lucia offered little resistance but Guadeloupe, their next objective, was a much tougher proposition, but by dint of surprise attacks, more use of cold steel with Edward always in the thick of it shouting encouragement to his men, it too fell to the English.

Now he was free to go back to Julie; to take up their harmonious life together again . . . and . . . please God . . . home to England. It was ten years since he had last lived in his native country. How long would he have to wait? In the meantime he must go back to Halifax.

.　　.　　.　　.　　.

As the frigate *Blanche* slowly made its way up to Halifax, Edward prayed for a miracle . . . that Julie would not yet have left Halifax. He knew it was but wishful thinking . . . but passages were hard to come by. There was just a slender hope. Now that the fighting was over, he longed for Julie's comforting presence. How long would he have to cool his heels in Halifax? Beyond being ordered to proceed to Halifax, he knew nothing.

Sir John Wentworth, as Lieutenant-General of Nova Scotia, was at the quay-side to meet him and as they greeted each other, Edward could not help noticing some uneasiness about the gentleman. It was not until they were in the carriage that Edward was able to ask, 'Madame de St. Laurent? When did she leave?'

He was totally unprepared for the answer, 'Only but yesterday, Sir. The sailings were so bad, that Madame was compelled to wait . . .'

'Oh, my God! Just a day out from Halifax when I arrive . . .'

'We had no knowledge of your impending arrival, Sir . . . We can write immediately so that she can come back straight away . . .'

'That is of no use . . . I do not know whether I am to go to England or to stay here. Have you not had any official notification?'

'Regretfully, Sir, no, but you know you are our most welcome guest until such times . . . May I say, Sir, how much we enjoyed the company of Madame de St. Laurent.

We found her the most charming, goodnatured . . .'

'Yes, yes, yes. That is why I wish to be reunited with her as quickly as possible . . . I think, after all, I will write her immediately.'

Halifax disgusted him. Within a few days of arrival, he had come to the conclusion that apart from being a naval base and a garrison, it was nothing more than a gigantic brothel. Sir John and Lady Frances continued to fuss and fawn over him, but knowing of the lady's reputation, he was wary of too much of their company. Accordingly, he decided to travel and see as much of Nova Scotia as possible while awaiting events.

. . . . .

Arriving in London, Julie lost no time in calling on Mr. Coutts. She found him to be a man of most genial disposition ready to help in any way he could. There was wonderful news from the West Indies. Martinique and St. Lucia were in the hands of the English. His Royal Highness had proved himself the most gallant officer.

Now all that remained was that Madame should enjoy her stay in London. Mr. Coutts would deem it an honour if she would accept the use of one of his coaches and his box at Drury Lane. She thanked him with smiling gratitude but uppermost in her mind was a desire to trace some of her émigré friends.

It was a difficult task, for most of them were living in straitened circumstances in poor shabby districts, only too glad that they had escaped with their lives. The Baron Fortisson, she learned, had rejoined the French army and was fighting out in the West Indies. She felt a momentary revulsion that one of her old friends should be Edward's enemy, bent on killing each other, but was not the fate of dear Phillipe-Claude more pitiable? No hero's death for him; the last news was that he was in the Carmes jail awaiting execution. Why oh why, had he left Malaga? That first Christmas in Gibraltar, Edward had been so happy, he had sent a gift of money to the Marquis as a token of good-will. Everywhere she went among the émigrés the story was the same; some of her dearest friends already guillo-tined . . . others waiting . .

All very well for Mr. Coutts to advise her to enjoy Lon-don. How could she? In the borrowed carriage, she took to driving past the gates of the Queen's House in the hope of seeing members of Edward's family. Eventually she was rewarded. What a wizened up little lady was the Queen! How in the world did she ever beget such beautiful daughters? And the Prince of Wales! How fat and florid! So different from Edward. One day, while out driving she was fortunate to see him in his carriage accompanied by a lady and on Philip Beck making enquiries was told she was Mrs. Fitzherbert. She too was plump but in a different way; kind and motherly looking.

Under the care of Philip Beck and her footman, she visited Ranelagh and Vauxhall, naughtily telling herself while she found London's night-life intoxicating, it would not be to Edward's fastidious taste.

She had been in London two weeks when Edward's letter arrived. She was in an ecstasy of joy, hastening round to Thomas Coutts' office. He was expecting her, having also received a note from Edward, and greeted her jovially.

'Ah, Madame, so you have come to arrange a passage back to Canada.'

'I have indeed, Sir. How soon?'

He shrugged his shoulders. 'That I cannot say with any exactitude, but leave it to me, dear lady. In the meantime, make the most of your remaining time in London.'

'Have you any news of His Highness' future?'

'Indeed I have. His Highness is to be given the command of the forces in Nova Scotia and New Brunswick. He is to be stationed in Halifax.'

She wanted to cry out at the injustice of it all, already feeling the hurt for Edward. How could his father be so cruel?

'Is the Prince yet acquainted with this order?'

'No, Madame, no. It will go with other government mail on the first ship available . . .'

'And that is the ship I, too, wish to travel by.'

Edward was alive and well and she was going back to rejoin him. He would need her comfort and love when he learned he was not to return to England. How she wished there was a sailing that very day.

She was roused by Mr. Coutts politely asking how she had enjoyed her stay . . . the shops . . . the theatre.

She suddenly brightened, asking, 'Will Mrs. Jordan be performing tonight?'

'Of a certainty. Now that she has fully recovered after the birth of her son, she is performing every night.'

A baby. She felt a pang of envy. She went to the play and came away with the image of a warm-hearted, jolly woman. She would have so much to tell Edward.

Not knowing what she would find in Halifax by way of silk mercers, she revelled in buying numerous dress lengths. She bought wigs, perfumes, books for Edward and presents for all the de Salaberry family.

As the *Westmoreland* packet set sail on July 9th her heart was singing. Given fair wind and weather, only another month before she was back in the arms of the man she so adored.

· · · · ·

From the deck, she could see him waiting on the quay-side. Dear, dear Edward. He must have been meeting every packet that came in during these last few weeks for he had no knowledge of her arrival. Impatiently, she took her turn down the gang-plank and then almost ran towards him and would have thrown herself into his arms . . . then she remembered . . . This man was His Royal Highness, Prince Edward. She made a full curtsey and as he raised her, a flicker of amusement played about his lips.

As soon as they were seated in the carriage, he took her hand, pressing it between his, murmuring, 'Thank God, Julie . . . thank God, you are back.'

      ·   ·   ·   ·   ·

They found a small mansion built of wood standing in its own grounds on Citadel Hill, near to the barracks. Together they visited the stores, buying furniture and drapes, planning the parties and assemblies they would hold, but Edward rarely discussing his disappointment.

Perhaps he vented his disappointment on his unfortunate troops, for having now received his new command and promotion, he once again put into action his harsh, vicious, sadistic training. It was the same pattern as before. Early parades and floggings for faults as small as a dirty button or being out of step.

Then in the evening, he was the cultured, gentle prince who disliked heavy drinking; who at Julie's request never allowed his guests to dally over their port more than fifteen minutes before joining the ladies. He never gambled, never played cards, but entertained in a still more lavish style than ever in Quebec; their guests being drawn from all walks of life, with Julie taking over from Frances Wentworth as the town's leading hostess.

It was obvious from the beginning that there was no love lost between the ladies. It was after one of their assemblies that Julie sought Edward's hearing.

'I do declare, Edward, Lady Frances Wentworth is the most detestable person I have ever met. Not only does she ogle every gentleman in the company, including you, but in her loud voice, she expressed her boredom of all our levées and assemblies. I am tempted to drop her from my invitation list.'

Edward laughed. 'That would never do, *ma fleur*. To cause a rift in our society would be an encouragement to dissatisfaction among the townspeople and the troops. They take their cue from us, and a more moderate way of living is just beginning to emerge. Be patient, Julie.'

'But she is so false . . . fair to my face, but talking against us behind our backs.'

'I know. I also know of the affair she had with my brother William several years ago; cuckolding her husband, but thus gaining his position and knighthood. I also understand that through my brother's influence she has been presented to the Queen . . . who loves flattery . . . and has consequently been made a lady-in-waiting with leave of absence . . . So you see, dearest . . .'

Julie nodded. 'Indeed I do, but if Lady Frances thinks I am inclined to follow her style of entertaining, allowing the gentlemen to join us in a drunken condition, telling us their lewd jokes and stories, she is doomed to disappointment. We, Edward, shall continue to be bores.'

Frances, however, had no intention of losing royal favour, continuing to toady to them whenever in their company. When he heard Julie discoursing on the disadvantages of living in the heart of Halifax, almost in the barracks, she was quick to come forward with a suggestion. She and her husband had a small house in the country, not too far from Halifax, with much spare land attached. If His Highness was interested, the land was his, and there he could build a house for dear, sweet Madame de St. Laurent.

Edward was all enthusiasm, and Julie, remembering Montmorency House, found herself in agreement, little as she liked accepting favours from Frances.

. . . . .

There was bad news from the West Indies. The French had recaptured Guadeloupe and what was more, it was reported they were massing troops ready to invade Canada.

Edward knew that everyone was looking to him. Now was his opportunity to use all the man-power Halifax could muster; idlers who made a living as best they could, legal or illegal, and Frenchmen taken prisoners in the various engagements and brought to Halifax to fend for themselves. Losing no time, Edward had them building battlements and moats. On the flat roof of the barracks, he had cannons positioned to cover the harbour in case of an attack from the sea. Food and ammunition to withstand a twelve months' siege was accumulated and stored away. More guns to cover the entrance to the harbour, a chain boom to deter all French vessels, more forts up and down the coast-line, some with furnaces to make shot so hot as to be an additional, menacing deterrent to the wooden, inflammable vessels. Let the French invaders come. They would get a hot reception.

All Canada waited. In the meantime, Edward's house at Fort Basin was completed. It was an exotic building; his own design, in Italian style, flat roofed, built of white wood, with a covered walk of columns and lattice work, over which a mass of climbing plants entwined themselves. Inside, the house boasted a large ballroom and dining-room. A separate building behind housed the kitchens, Edward's office and a guard-room! In front of the house was a bandstand where the regimental band played every Sunday afternoon after the regiment, with Edward at its head, had paraded in full dress uniform through the streets of Halifax.

A gravel path twisted its incongruous way between shrubs and bushes spelling out 'Julie' and leading to a Chinese temple from which came the tinkle of bells as the wind whispered through hanging copper wafer-like chimes.

A brook, embellished with several dashing, splashing waterfalls, babbled its way to a lake, cut to the shape of a heart, passing numerous little arbours, all furnished with seats, all tinkling merrily from glass chimes suspended from their roofs.

Edward and Halifax still awaited the threatened invasion. To while away the tedium, when not with the troops, Edward became fascinated with any mechanical device based on the uncoiling spring. He began a collection of clocks, musical boxes, clockwork animals and birds that could perform all manner of movement. So big did his collection grow, that a special servant was detailed to their regular winding.

* * * * *

Edward had again written to his father, the occasion being the impending resignation of Lord Dorchester, governor of Lower Canada. Did his father not consider he had earned that position, judging by his active service in the West Indies and his fortification of Halifax?

In the meantime, news-sheets out of England were full of the marriage of the Prince of Wales to his cousin, Caroline of Brunswick, and what was more, the Princess was already *enceinte*. The news left him cold. It would seem that he did not belong to the Royal Family. None of his brothers or sisters ever wrote to him nowadays.

How long would it be before he received his father's answer . . . if indeed he bothered to reply?

* * * * *

It was many months before the answer came and then to say the appointment had been given to eighty-year-old Major-General Robert Prescott. At first Edward was deeply mortified that he could be passed over for a doddering old octogenarian, and it took much of Julie's tact and patience to restore his equanimity, so that she was delighted when

Lieutenant Charles de Salaberry arrived unexpectedly in Halifax with his regiment. He had joined the British army at sixteen as Edward's protégé and now Julie was amazed at the warmth of Edward's affection, for he could not have shown more delight had it been his own son . . .

Though his arrival stirred up all her suppressed longings, she showed no chagrin. Indeed his companionship was having such a beneficial effect on Edward that she doubly welcomed the boy, and soon they were all enjoying special parties given for him and his fellow-officers. There were gay skating-parties on the frozen, heart-shaped lake, with the grounds lit by fairy lights strung from tree to tree, and the band in the distance playing lilting waltzes. There were sled races for the more adventurous, and shooting and hunting.

When the news came of the birth of Princess Charlotte, Edward's comment was a mere laconic, 'Pity it wasn't a boy. Still I expect there'll be more.'

'Why is it a pity?' asked Julie with a touch of humour.

'England needs a strong man on the throne . . . not a woman full of fanciful ideas . . .'

'I have heard much of your Queen Elizabeth . . .'

'Maybe . . . but consider the state of my father's reign . . . a king suffering from madness . . . yet I doubt if there will be another child, for the news-sheets state with authority that the Prince and Princess of Wales have parted . . .'

'How dreadful! So soon! Oh Edward, it must be wicked gossip . . .'

Soon, however, with more news-sheets arriving, the truth was only too evident. Edward was quick to express his disgust. Apparently, his brother had been in the arms of his mistress, Lady Jersey, before the marriage, and almost immediately after the wedding night.

. . . . . .

91

The note delivered by courier was brief. Julie smiled. Never a week went by without a similar happening. His Royal Highness was bringing three gentlemen to dinner. Beyond setting three extra places, no trouble was involved, for Julie's house-keeping prepared for any eventuality. She was accustomed to entertaining gentlemen of all ranks, but when Edward presented her to them, she immediately sank into a curtsey, eyes downcast, glad of the opportunity to hide her rising colour. His Royal Highness the Duc D'Orleans and his two brothers! She had met them all, danced with them in those gay days of the Marquis de Permangle. Louis raised her up, kissing her hand with true French finesse. It was a gay meal despite the story they had to tell; their flight from France with little more than what they stood up in . . . no money . . . no jewels for sale . . .

'How then do you intend to exist, Sir?' Julie asked.

'Do not laugh, Madame. We intend, provided we can find some beneficent creditor, to open a school. Who better to teach the French language? Swordsmanship? Riding? All the things a gentleman should learn . . .'

'An excellent idea!' It was Edward, '. . . and my dear young sirs, why should I not be that creditor?'

'You mean it, Sir?'

'If a loan of £200 would be of assistance . . .'

'A veritable fortune, Sir. But it must be only a loan . . .'

·   ·   ·   ·   ·

Julie gave a scream of terror when she saw the men carrying the improvised stretcher. Edward. What had happened? Was he dead?

They were quick to assure her that His Highness was only hurt, and that the army doctor had been sent for. His horse had stumbled while crossing a make-shift bridge, throwing him heavily. She gazed down at the big bruise on his forehead and listened with dread to his repeated, tight-lipped moans of, 'My back. Oh my God, my back. I believe it's broken.'

His back was not broken, but badly bruised, necessitating rest in bed. Julie was the most conscientious and devoted of nurses, but when several weeks went by without the patient showing any desire to leave his bed, she became alarmed, and tackled him as to his lack of co-operation with the doctor.

To her surprise, a slow smile passed over his face. 'Lying here, I have had much time to think, *ma petite . . .*'

'And what have you been thinking, *mon brave?*'

'Just how much I want to go to England. Will you help me, Julie?'

'How?'

'When the doctor comes tomorrow, start a conversation about the various spas throughout Europe, mentioning those where you know remarkable cures have been effected. I am interested in only one place, Bath, in England, but we must be subtle in handling the conversation.' He took her hand in his. 'It's worth trying, is it not, *ma petite?*'

She laughed joyously. 'You schemer, Edward, and there I was, visualising you on your back for the rest of your life. Will I help? Anything for you, *mon chéri*. Anything.'

•   •   •   •   •

The ruse had worked. After many consultations, followed by numerous medical reports being sent to England, with all the doctors recommending the remedial waters of Bath, His Majesty King George III had at last graciously decided to invite his son Edward to return to England. Edward and Julie were filled with joy.

No time was lost in packing, for a British warship was already on its way to carry them across the Atlantic. The voyage took four weeks but they were both so engrossed in their anticipation, so full of plans for their new life, so much to talk about that the time passed quickly. How wonderful if they were in England in time for Christmas, but here, Edward felt he must warn Julie. He would be expected to accept all invitations from the various members of his family and though it cut him to the heart, he would not be able to have her accompany him.

Julie smiled bravely. 'Sir, please do not concern yourself unduly. I would never wish to embarrass you. 'Tis fourteen years is it not since you saw your mother and sisters, while I have had the pleasure of your company all these years ...'

'Don't mistake me, my darling,' he interrupted quickly, 'I shall be with you on every possible occasion. When I am away from you, you must regard it as though I was away on duty. I shall be given a suite of rooms in one of the palaces, but we shall find a house where we can live our private lives in the same way as we have done all these years.'

She knew then that from now onwards the pattern of their lives would change; now more than ever, she must keep in the background, but so long as their love remained constant, she would be happy.

5

Edward was amazed at the reception awaiting him when
the ship docked at Portsmouth. After being ignored for so
many years, he had never expected either a family or a civic
welcome.

Yet there it was; the bunting and the decorations; the
band; the cheering crowd yelling itself hoarse while guns
boomed out their welcome. Discreetly Julie kept in the
background while His Worship the Mayor and his aldermen
gave Edward the freedom of the borough. Then it was that
he noticed the lady standing beside the Mayor . . . none
other than Frances, Lady Wentworth. The ceremony completed, she stepped over to him and after a brief greeting
led the way to a veritable cavalcade of awaiting vehicles,
all bearing the royal coat-of-arms, Julie rejoining Edward,
with eyebrows raised in surprise. They were aware that Her
Ladyship had preceded them to England, ostensibly to
take her son to school, but never expected that she would
be sent by Their Majesties to welcome home their son, after
an absence of fourteen years.

She was all efficiency and bustle. She and Edward and
Julie in the first carriage, Edward's valet and Julie's maid
in the second, while she herself supervised the packing of
the baggage wagon.

'I know these ship-porters,' she said tartly as she took
her place in the carriage, 'so easy to whip away small bags
when there is such a vast amount.' She looked first at Julie

and then at Edward, smiling benignly. 'Welcome home to England. I expect it feels good, Sir, does it not?'

Edward shook his head, unable at first to find his voice, then, 'It is a wonderful moment, Madame. I cannot express my feelings.'

'Then don't try, Sir. Let me tell you of the arrangements. Their Majesties and the Princesses are at Windsor, and you, Sir, are requested to visit them tomorrow.'

'My father? His state of health?'

'Much better. Of course, he is very frail and his mind is apt to wander, but not alarmingly so. His conversation is quite sensible and he is aware of all immediate matters.'

'And my sisters? I read in the news-sheets that the Princess Charlotte had last year married the King of Wurttemberg, but none wrote me the details. The others? Are none of them betrothed? Augusta will be thirty . . . surely . . .'

'Ah, that is one of His Majesty's oddities. He idolises his daughters. Thinks none of their would-be suitors good enough . . .'

'The Princess Charlotte was fortunate then to escape? And my little sister Amelia? She was but twelve months old when I left England . . .'

'She is a most beautiful girl, Your Highness, as indeed they all are. You will be charmed by them.' She looked across at Julie. 'You are quiet, Madame.'

'. . . but I am listening . . . learning, become acquainted with the Prince's family.'

'I have told Their Majesties and the Princesses much about you . . .'

'You have?' The ejaculation came in unison from Edward and Julie.

'Do not pester yourselves,' was the laughing rejoinder, 'I have reported nothing but good, extolling Madame's virtue, and her loving concern for their son.'

Julie was undecided as to whether Her Ladyship was being sarcastic or sincere, and accordingly decided to pursue another line of conversation. 'Could you enlighten us as to where we shall be staying until we find a suitable house?'

'Of course. With me. A suite of rooms at Kensington Palace has been put at the disposal of the Prince, but while he will be conducting his business from there, I am sure he will not wish to pass the nights alone.' She winked broadly at Edward before going on, 'And tomorrow, while His Highness is at Windsor, I will present you to certain of my friends who are already anticipating the honour; the business of finding a house can wait until after Christmas.'

Edward eyed her warily. 'I would have you choose all acquaintances for Madame de St. Laurent with great care . . .'

'As if I did not know, Sir. To begin with, Mrs. Fitzherbert . . .'

'Excellent. Excellent. How is the dear lady?'

Frances Wentworth hesitated. 'She is in excellent health, Sir, but somewhat perturbed. His Royal Highness, the Prince of Wales, is anxious that they should renew their old . . . that she should return to him . . .'

'God forbid,' Edward exploded . . . 'after his callous treatment . . . his mistress, Lady Jersey . . .'

'That is now over, Sir. All day long, the Prince goes around sobbing and sighing for his Maria . . .'

'But he has a wife . . .'

'So Mrs. Fitzherbert reminds him, but he refuses to listen. I think she is contemplating going abroad.'

'I must visit her at the earliest opportunity. She was most kind to me when I dashed over from Geneva . . . but the Princess of Wales? What news of her?'

'She is enjoying life, Sir, as never before! She has her own establishment, gives lavish parties and assemblies and has a host of gentlemen admirers. I quite envy her.' She smiled wantonly at Edward, then admonished herself. 'No I don't. Now that I am turned fifty, I have decided to be the perfect, well-behaved wife. You should have heard what your brother William said, when I made the same remark to him.'

Edward had no wish to hear what form of obscenity William's observation had taken, and hurriedly asked, 'How is he? And Mrs. Jordan?'

Frances' peal of laughter reverberated round the confines of the carriage. 'Dear Mrs. Jordan is about to present him with a fourth child . . . just imagine, four!' As her laughter died away, so the silence in the carriage took its place. 'Four children,' thought Julie. 'All loved and wanted.' 'Four children,' thought Edward. 'William always was a fool. No wonder the lampoons mocked him and Mrs. Jordan. No sense of discretion. No dignity.'

He knew that the conversation was not to Julie's taste, but if Frances Wentworth was to be their hostess over the Christmas season, it would not do to antagonise her. Deep down, she was being kind; it was just that she could not altogether suppress her wanton outlook.

'The other children?' Julie queried gently. 'Boys or girls?'

'Two boys and one girl. Anyone ready to wager as to the sex of number four?' As there was no reply, she went on blithely, 'I wonder how many more, Sir? Great man for the ladies is the Duke as you well know.'

'I understand he is most happily domiciled with Mrs. Jordan,' came Edward's stiff retort.

'So he is . . . but . . .' again the bubbling laughter, 'Mrs. Jordan is away from home so much on her theatrical tours . . . Can you blame the Duke?'

By the time they reached London, Frances had run out of news and gossip and the latter part of the journey was passed in comparative silence, for which Julie was thankful. She was beginning to feel apprehensive at the prospect of meeting so many new acquaintances; avoiding gossip and scandal, but above all, being a credit to Edward. She must not fail him.

.   .   .   .   .

Whenever Julie looked back to the Christmas of 1798, it was to recall a mad sequence of balls, assemblies, dinners and dances, first at one aristocratic house and then another; being presented to a host of over-obsequious, flattering gentlemen and hawk-eyed, critical, over-dressed or under-dressed ladies. Never before had she been so grateful for the strict social grooming that had been part of her education.

Edward had returned from Windsor full of his reception. His parents had been wonderfully kind, never mentioning the past grievances, while his sisters were surely the most beautiful girls in England. What was more, they were all most desirous of meeting Madame Julie de St. Laurent.

As with Catherine de Salaberry, so an immediate friendship sprang into being between Julie and Maria Fitzherbert. Again, perhaps it was because they were both Catholics, but there were other common factors. They were both in love with a prince . . . brothers. 'Oh yes,' Maria confessed when, greetings over, they quickly reached the subject uppermost in all their minds, oh yes, she still loved George . . . she would love him to the end of her days . . . but return to him . . . no. Now at least she had peace. No drunken, brawling husband; no more public humiliations. Yet Julie could detect the heartache, and when taking her leave, was not surprised at Maria's whispered, 'Come again soon. Alone, so that we can talk.'

The Prince of Wales and his Carlton House cronies had already gone to Brighton for the season, but there was an urgent invitation that Edward and Julie should visit him there.

The luxurious, ostentatious settings and furnishings of

the Pavilion amazed them both, and Edward felt the old resentment stirring within him. When he had built the house at Bedford Basin, he had endeavoured to incorporate more taste, more luxury than he had observed during his short stay at Carlton House ten years ago. Now it would seem George was still well ahead of him.

His brother was all flattery to Julie, seeking her sympathy when telling them of Maria's cruelty towards him; begging Julie and Edward to plead his case.

As they expected, his brother Frederick, Duke of York, was also at the Pavilion, but not the Duchess Frederica, Maria having already told them that they had parted. One guest who charmed them both was the little Princess Charlotte, now nearly three years old. She was a lively, high-spirited child, obviously spoilt by everyone; including her grandmother and her aunts.

When news came that Mrs. Jordan had given birth, on the nineteenth of December, to another daughter, George insisted on a celebration, which ended in his copious weeping, envious of his brothers William and Edward, so fortunate to have the love of good women.

They did not remain long in Brighton, as it was necessary that they found a house in town, finally being successful in securing one in Knightsbridge. While the house was in the hands of decorators, they took the opportunity of driving over to Bushey to visit William and his family.

As their carriage pulled up at the steps of the house, the door opened and a small boy and girl came running down, followed by William holding a toddler of about two by the hand. Julie drew in her breath involuntarily. This was how family life should be.

Then Edward was presenting her, and William was introducing the children, George and Sophia already squabbling as to who should hold Julie's hand, with Henry retreating behind his papa, overcome by shyness.

She liked the look of William. Not so handsome as

Edward, or indeed any of the brothers, but this plump, round face radiated happiness and contentment.

'Come in. Come in. I forbade Mrs. Jordan to come out in the raw air so soon after her lying-in. Come in. My dear Dora is all impatience to meet you . . . and to show you our new daughter.'

Dorothy Jordan was standing within the room and as the gentlemen entered she sank into a curtsey before Edward, who was quick to raise her, leading her to a sofa.

'You should not be on your feet, Ma'am, so soon . . .'

'La, Sir. Within a few weeks I shall be back on the stage. The sooner I find my feet the better.'

He had feared to find another Duleque in Dorothy Jordan, but here was no tawdry actress, but a plump, motherly woman, obviously the heart of her family. When she spoke, her voice was punctuated by a suggestion of a warm, soft chuckle. William was indeed a fortunate man.

The children were romping around the room, unrestrained by their parents. William had pulled the bell asking that the new baby should be brought down and for the first time meeting all Edward's relations, Julie felt a moment of fear, having to see, probably hold, a new-born child. Somehow, she found the strength to take the little mite in her arms, to compliment the proud parents, all the time aware that Edward was now sharing the children's romps.

William watched with amusement. 'You should have a family yourself, Edward.'

Edward ceased his frolicking, gazing straight at his brother. 'Madame and I have no desire for children.'

When Julie next saw Maria, both ladies took the opportunity to ease their hearts.

'Dear Mrs. Fitzherbert, I cannot understand his denial. If you could but guess the heaviness of my heart each time I see or handle some other woman's child . . .'

'I understand.' She spoke so quietly, so decisively, that Julie looked at her in surprise.

101

'You . . . you too?'

Maria nodded. 'Yes, but in my case it was necessary. At the time I agreed willingly. No child of mine could succeed to the throne even though George, their father, would some day be King . . . and so . . . so . . . I promised that I would part with any child . . .' Her voice broke while tears streamed down her face, but within seconds, she was wiping them away, finding new strength in her voice to say with emphasis, 'But with you it's different. Edward is so far down the line of succession, there is no fear . . . especially as Princess Charlotte is now the direct heir. William is not in the least concerned, proud of his brood, as you would see . . .'

'But as brothers they are totally different, are they not? William, happy-go-lucky, indifferent as to what the world says. Edward so proud; so dignified.'

'Pooh! fat lot of good his pride and dignity has done him so far. Yet you're in love with him, are you not, dear Julie?'

     ·   ·   ·   ·   ·

By March they were comfortably installed in the house at Knightsbridge, in good time to hold a grand assembly to celebrate Edward's long awaited dukedom. Now he was the Duke of Kent and Strathearn, and Earl of Dublin with an annual allowance from the government of £12,000.

With Julie by his side, he welcomed his guests; his brothers and the cream of the aristocracy. They were curious about the new duke, who had left the country a mere boy, and had come back a man of thirty-one. They were curious about Madame de St. Laurent. There were rumours that they were married, yet all were well aware of the restrictions of the Royal Marriage Act; but they took an instant liking to the gay, witty French lady, so different from the dour duke.

102

Edward considered he had reasons to be dour. Why had he been kept waiting for his dukedom when the Duke of York received his at twenty-one, the Duke of Clarence at twenty-three, the Duke of Cumberland at twenty-eight, and now at the same time as himself his younger brother, Augustus, had been made Duke of Cambridge? There was no justice. Then there was the question of those equipments that had been lost at sea or captured by the French, five in all, at a cost of over £10,000. Surely, since they were lost on active service, the government should compensate him. And why should William have an extra allowance for the maintenance of his establishment? His debts in Gibraltar, which should have been paid long ago with interest, had not been paid after all, despite his father's promise.

He had now arranged that part of his £12,000 a year should go to liquidating his debts.

Then to his pleasurable surprise, he learned the inhabitants of Halifax had raised five hundred guineas and purchased a diamond star in recognition of his services to Nova Scotia, the collection being organised by Sir John Wentworth.

'And what did I do in Nova Scotia?' he demanded of Julie in good-tempered sarcasm.

'Why . . . you fortified it against invasion . . . you gave employment to the down-and-outs . . . you made Halifax a place fit to live in . . . to walk about with safety . . . you somehow brought the people together . . . they became fond of you . . .'

'Spare my blushes, Madame. Sir John hasn't gone to all this trouble without a motive, a motive no doubt dictated by Lady Frances. Just you wait and see.'

There was an imposing ceremony at Kensington Palace when young Charles Wentworth, Frances' elder son, presented the star to His Royal Highness, whereupon the King, much impressed, gave the young man a post on His Majesty's Council in Nova Scotia.

Back at Knightsbridge, Edward could not refrain from laughingly reminding Julie, 'I told you so. The Wentworths do not cast their bread upon the water unless they know there's rich plum cake in the offing.' But there was a certain panache about him. There was promotion for him too. He had been appointed Commander-in-Chief of British Forces in North America.

. . . . .

With total disregard of expense, Edward ordered another equipment, compatible with his new post, this time costing £11,000 and containing five thousand books!

It was only at the last minute that they realised Edward as yet had not taken any treatment at Bath! Quickly they made good the omission, for the army doctors would require details of the cure!

Another surprise awaited them when they called to take leave of Mrs. Fitzherbert. She too was packing and judging by the dust-sheet-covered furniture, it looked as though she meant being out of London for some considerable time.

She was most apologetic for the state of confusion, but over a dish of tea, said haltingly, 'I suppose you will think me a fool . . . but . . . but I am considering returning to George.'

'The devil you are!' ejaculated Edward. 'After his callous treatment . . . his repeated insults . . .'

'I know. I know . . . but . . .'

'Are you returning to him straight away? Going to Brighton . . . ?'

'Oh no. No. As yet I have given no definite promise. It depends upon the Pope . . .' She stopped suddenly, realising that she was about to betray the secret of her marriage. 'Don't ask me any more, Sir. I beg of you . . .'

Julie gave Edward a warning glance. They had heard

rumours of a marriage, just as they knew their own union was discussed.

* * * * * *

William insisted on seeing them aboard the *Arethusa*. He was cock-a-hoop, full of high spirits. His dear Mrs. Jordan was again *enceinte*.

Edward waited until his brother had gone ashore before giving vent to the absurdity of William's behaviour. Soon to be five illegitimate children! When would he learn sense?

Julie was on a see-saw of emotions; sad to be uprooted from her new friends, but glad for Edward, for this was a post he had always coveted, and after all, they were going home to their lovely house outside Halifax . . . and to the dear, dear de Salaberrys.

* * * * *

It was a dismal beginning to his new post to learn that the transport *Recovery*, carrying all his new equipment, had been captured by the French. To think of the enemy handling his personal belongings riled him far more than if they were resting on the bed of the ocean.

There was nothing for it but to order another equipment; an equipment of similar value.

Now he began to put into motion various projects he had had in mind, during his previous stay in Halifax; a new barracks; a new hospital; a house for his senior general; a new, more palatial house for the Wentworths. Little wonder Sir John Wentworth's letters to England continued to eulogise the Duke!

The natural outcome of all this building was the improvement in the living conditions of the working people. Their houses took on a new look; and all around Halifax, the wealthy set about building mansions for themselves.

No longer now did Edward rise with the dawn to inspect his troops, but nevertheless he was at his desk from dawn till midnight; despite the fact that he had a secretary and five under-secretaries! He himself dealt with every letter, every order, even those of smallest detail, before handing them on, with his comments.

Julie was deeply concerned about his health. He had so little time for sleep, so little exercise, and now he was complaining of stomach pains and biliousness. Throughout the long winter months they had both suffered from colds and bronchitis. If only the Duke would slow down, enjoy a little leisure, she felt sure they would both improve.

Edward had hoped that Monsieur de Salaberry would be made his aide-de-camp, which would have meant the de Salaberrys residing in Halifax, so much desired by Julie. With the government's refusal, however, the best the Duke could do for his friend was to have him appointed Superintendent of the Red Indians.

.   .   .   .   .

It was almost unbelievable! So fantastic, that one equipment after another should be lost, but here was the news that the *Frances*, conveying the latest to be ordered, had been wrecked, a total loss, on Sable Island.

Edward's spirits sank. It would seem he was doomed to live in sparse, bare surroundings, devoid of all the trappings of a cultured gentleman . . . of a royal duke. He was overwhelmed by a wave of home-sickness.

Julie was all sympathy. 'Anything you wish, *mon brave*, I am with you. Canada or England.'

He spoke what had been in his mind for some time. 'Now that the union of Great Britain and Ireland becomes law on the first of January next year, a commander-in-chief will have to be appointed . . .'

'And you, Sir, would welcome the appointment?'

'I would indeed. Do you not consider I have all the necessary qualities? An experienced soldier . . . a man of the
people . . .'

'Indeed, Sir, yes, and what I consider most important,
your sympathy with the Roman Catholics. You have had
most happy relations with them here.'

He smiled at her. 'So true, Madame, so very true. I will
mention all this to my father.'

'You are going to write to him? To ask to return?'

'I am. It is a great disappointment to me that I have not
had the honour of being Governor of Canada. Perhaps
higher honour awaits me at home.' He was silent for a
moment, then, 'England is also facing the threat of invasion.
Napoleon's power on the Continent has almost reached its
peak. That is something else I must stress in my letter; that
I am prepared to take up any responsible military post . . .
but I feel sure that I shall be Commander-in-Chief of
Ireland.'

.   .   .   .   .   .

His letter had been received and answered with all graci-
ousness. Edward and Madame Julie de St. Laurent could
return to England, the *Assistance* being put at their disposal.

On August 3rd 1800, Julie, from the vantage point of the
de Salaberry carriage, watched Edward march down to the
ship. Despite his recent ill-health, how smart he looked at
the head of his troops; not cold and grim as was his wont,
but bowing and smiling to the citizens lining the streets,
who had come to bid him farewell, for he and Madame had
now been in Canada for nearly ten years.

What an excellent officer he was! How different today
were the troops; smart, upright, uniforms immaculate; even
their hair cut to a standard style!

And was he not a goodly man, his last public duty being

the laying of foundation stones for both a church and a Freemasons' hall?

But the troops marching behind the Duke felt only elation. With his going, there would come a relaxation of discipline. Oh yes, he was a kind, generous man. Had he not reprieved eight of the eleven men under sentence of death for desertion and mutiny?

There was a touching farewell with the de Salaberrys. When would they meet again? Of course they would correspond as before, and their sons would be visiting them in England . . . especially young Edward, their godson, for the Duke was going to be his patron, having promised him a commission in the British army.

6

Arriving in London at the end of August, it was to find that Their Majesties, the Princesses and all the Court had gone to Weymouth, its peace and quietness being prescribed by the doctors as necessary for the King, whose condition was again giving rise to anxiety.

Edward decided to lose no time. If he wanted that post in Ireland, now was the opportunity to ask his father outright. Did Julie object to being left in Knightsbridge? He could not take her to Court without invitation.

'Of course not, *mon chéri*. There is so much to do here. I am longing to visit dear Mrs. Fitzherbert . . .' She laughed mischievously, 'to find out how much of the gossip is true.'

The ladies' reunion was interspersed with laughter and tears. '*Ma chère* Maria, how charming, how radiant you look . . .'

'*Ah, Julie, ma petite, c'est l'amour . . .*'

They both laughed. 'We heard that you and the Prince of Wales . . .' began Julie.

' 'Tis true . . . and we are happy, so very, very happy.'

'Then I am happy for you.' Julie hesitated, '. . . and about . . . is it true also . . . that . . . ?'

'So you have heard? That we have a baby? She is the child of my very dear friends, the Seymours. I am but caring for her while her parents, both in ill-health, have gone abroad in search of a cure.'

'. . . and I warrant enjoying every moment of it. But be warned, dear Maria; don't become too involved or you will find it hard to part. Incidentally, it was another son, was it not, that Mrs. Jordan presented to the Duke last January?'

'It would appear all news reaches Canada. Have you also heard that Mrs. Jordan is again . . . ?'

'No, no, no,' laughed Julie. 'Poor Mrs. Jordan.'

'I don't know. Sometimes I envy her. Sometimes I think . . . but this is absurd talk. How is dear Edward?'

'Much better, much happier now that he is in England. Ah, I nearly forgot. He asked me to enquire about your house at Castle Hill. Is it still on the market?'

'But of a certainty. I was determined none but the Duke should have the house.'

'Then he asks that you will put the sale into motion so that no time is lost. We need a bigger residence than our Knightsbridge house. And now, dear Maria, do you think I might have a peep at the baby?'

Mrs. Fitzherbert pulled the bell-rope. 'I was hoping you would ask. Had you not asked I should still have inflicted the child on you. I am so proud of her,' she laughed.

As Julie held the little girl in her arms, all the old heart-ache returned. She mustn't dwell on such thoughts. Brusquely, she asked, 'The Prince of Wales? How does he respond to having a child in the house?'

Maria beamed. 'He absolutely dotes on her. Simply dotes on her.'

* * * * *

It was most unfortunate that the Weymouth breezes did not have the desired effect on the King's mentality. Edward found his father to be totally incapable of carrying on a satisfactory conversation. Whenever he mentioned Ireland, his father's face was a complete blank, merely rolling his head with alarming rapidity. The doctors insisted that Edward speak no more of government matters, and that the King return to London with as little delay as possible.

Edward was only too glad to return to Julie, the one person to whom he could speak freely; the one person who could give him ease when his mind was so sorely tried. He would have to seek the help of his brothers, George the Prince of Wales, and Frederick, who was now Commander-in-Chief of the British army.

To Edward's surprise, he found Frederick recalcitrant, unfriendly and as the weeks went by discovered that George was being influenced by him. It was to Maria that he poured out his troubles. Did she know what had gone wrong?

Maria hesitated. It was commonplace now for both George and the Duke to speak disparagingly of Edward, laughing and scoffing at his prim and dignified bearing.

'Well, Sir, I think the Duke's animosity is due to his jealousy.'

'Jealousy? And why should he be jealous?'

'Because of your prowess in the West Indies; your excellent work in Canada . . . and his recent failure in the Netherlands . . . kow-towing to Bonaparte! 'Tis clear to see, you have not read the vilifications of the press . . .' She lowered her voice. 'But I beg of you, Sir, make no mention of what has passed between us.'

So that was it. No use expecting either George or Frederick to further his progress.

* * * * *

While Frederica, Duchess of York, remained firm in her refusal to meet either Mrs. Fitzherbert, Mrs. Jordan or Madame de St. Laurent, on the score it would be lowering her dignity as a Prussian princess, Caroline, Princess of Wales, was only too glad to welcome any of them who called on her, even Maria who was now again living with her husband! Indeed, she had on more than one occasion turned to Mrs. Fitzherbert for help and advice. Caroline had been much mortified when the Prince had appointed Colonel Thomas to act as her auditor, despite her own admission that her monetary affairs were in a deplorable state. Now after several months of Colonel Thomas' administration, her accounts appeared to be more confused than ever. She was convinced he had no knowledge of book-keeping; George had put him into her house to spy on her. The next time she met Maria, she was voluble in her accusation.

In an endeavour to help, Mrs. Fitzherbert suggested to George that Edward, being a disinterested person, should examine the accounts. Edward, having time on his hands, was only too glad to accept George's commission, scrutinising all Caroline's bills and accounts with his customary efficiency. He was shocked at his discoveries. Colonel Thomas must go, he advised his brother. His services were useless.

To his amazement, George turned on him in a fury. Who was he to suggest Colonel Thomas' dismissal? It was the Princess of Wales who had put him up to it. Colonel Thomas stayed where he was, and what was more, he had no further wish to see Edward at any time.

Julie shook her head in dismay. ' 'Twould have been wiser, Sir, to have refused the task. Interference never has happy results.'

Now it was his turn to seek Maria's help, writing to her :

'I really felt it a duty to point out that the Colonel was in every respect unfit for the business . . . I trust it will need no great exertion to convince the Prince of my zeal in his service . . . I am apprehensive that it may put him in a little ill humour with me. Permit me, therefore, to hope you will assist me in convincing the Prince that I have acted only from the sense of duty.'

To gratify his dearest Maria, George pretended to forgive Edward, but deep down he determined to watch out for any further interference from this so-upright brother of his.

Meanwhile Julie and Edward were busy with the re-decoration and re-furnishing of Castle Hill Lodge. No expense was being spared, either in or outside the house. Castle Hill was to be their palace. His manservants had to be immaculate at all times. He kept a resident hairdresser to attend to their hair; a resident tailor to see to the perfect fit of their uniforms. They were put on parade every morning, Edward inspecting them for any fault. A servant stayed up all night to keep the fire going in his master's room; to be ready to serve him with a cup of coffee promptly at five o'clock.

Each day, after breakfast, the housekeeper had to present to him an account of the previous day's expenditure; each day an army of women servants went from room to room, dusting and re-dusting.

Then the renovations came to a sudden halt, for early in 1802 he was, to his great amazement, invited to become the Governor of Gibraltar, in place of Major-General Sir Charles O'Hara, who had now died.

Mr. Addington, the Prime Minister, was frank with Edward. *'The garrison is in a deplorable state, Sir. Drunkenness and mutiny. This state of affairs cannot be permitted to endure. It has lasted already too long. It must be put down, and Your Royal Highness is the man to do it. You may reckon on the support of the Cabinet at home.'*

Edward was cautious. He could recall the state of the Rock, all those years ago.

'As to the second in command, Barnett. Can I depend on him?'

'True as steel, rely on him.'

The command in Ireland had not materialised; he was at loggerheads with his two elder brothers; he despised their lecherous mode of living; he would be glad to get out of the country. Castle Hill Lodge would have to be closed, but it would be there awaiting them when he returned triumphantly from cleaning up the Rock.

Julie as usual was all acquiescence.

As they sailed away from England, Edward again perused the letter Frederick had sent him on his acceptance of the post.

'*I consider it my duty to make Your Royal Highness aware that much exertion will be necessary to establish a due degree of discipline among the troops,*' but went on to say, '*accomplish the reforms gradually.*'

He was also recalling his father's last words. '*Now, Sir, when you go to Gibraltar, do not make such a trade of it as when you went to Halifax.*'

Just what did they mean? Did they want the Rock cleaning up, or didn't they?

Reclining in the luxury of Carlton House, Frederick smirked gleefully, 'Well, that's put paid to Joseph Surface, the sanctimonious prig. Just wait and see, George. Soon there'll be all Hell let loose.'

'It was a clever ruse of yours, Fred, to cause him to think he was being honoured . . .'

'Honoured? He'll have no honour left when next he leaves Gibraltar. I'll put him in his place. He'll never outshine me again.'

'How long do you give the poor devil?'

Frederick studied the toes of his highly-polished boots . . . 'Twelve months. Yes. Twelve months at the most.'

.   .   .   .   .

Their arrival at the Rock coincided with the date they had formerly left it for Canada. May 10th. Exactly eleven years ago.

All the garrison were out to greet him; some on parade, others lining the route to the Convent, the official residence of the Governor of Gibraltar. Having been warned, Edward was quite prepared to find the troops in need of strict training, but never had he expected them to be so dissolute

. . . so degenerate looking . . . slovenly beyond all expression.

Parade was ordered for the next morning at three-thirty! The Duke of Kent had taken up the gauntlet.

After the parade, and defaulters had been taken to the punishment cells, there was the civilian court to attend, where three Spaniards awaited trial on a charge of stealing £500. Found guilty, Edward had no compunction in having them hanged. Civilians and troops alike were going to feel and fear his authority.

*   *   *   *   *

He had found a small house on the edge of Cork Woods, where Julie could stay when she became overwhelmed by the military parades, the floggings and the civil court trials, or even to get away from the drunken randyism of Gibraltar itself. Drunken soldiers rolled along its streets, until seized upon by evil-faced prostitutes; women devoid of all feminine attributes, save the one that secured their livelihood. There were ninety wineshops on the Rock; a rock that measured less than two square miles! Governor O'Hara had reaped a rich reward from the licence fees of these shops, £7,000 in all. Although it meant forfeiting much of this extra income, Edward ordered the closure of fifty of them, and the remainder were placed out of bounds for the troops. In their place, he built a brewery, and then licensed inns to supply the beer, but even then, men of different ranks must not drink together.

During the Summer, officers and men had to parade at three-thirty, an hour later in Spring and Autumn, and two hours later in Winter. There was a full dress parade during the morning and another in the evening. Roll was called at every meal time. A gun was fired every evening . . . a curfew which meant all men must be in barracks. More rules. More regulations. More punishments for those who dared to disobey or disregard.

Even their personal appearance came under the whip. Men must not grow whiskers. Their beards must be trimmed to regulation level. Hair must be cut regularly, only a limited amount of powder to be applied . . . and officers must cease their ridiculous custom of carrying umbrellas!

Despite his efforts to curb the drunkenness, which he blamed for most of the other prevalent crime, he was horrified at the amount of rape and attacks on women. Heavy penalties of flogging were always inflicted, whenever the culprits were traced.

In the middle of November, regiments fresh from the fighting in Egypt arrived at the Rock, expecting rest and relaxation. Instead they discovered that the Governor saw in them more troops to be inculcated with a higher standard of perfection. The flogging sheds housed more victims than ever.

Edward and Julie were preparing for Christmas. There were to be several big assemblies at the Convent, while smaller, more intimate dinner-parties were to be enjoyed at the Cork Woods house.

It was while Edward was on one of his tours of inspection that the first warning came. He had visited every section of the barracks, his eagle eye missing nothing.

He was inspecting the hospital when passing down between the straw palliasses placed on the floor, he noticed a sick man endeavouring to attract his attention. Going over and bending down, he listened to the man's whisper. 'Sire. There is a plot to murder you. They intend to seize you on Christmas Eve.'

Edward waited. There were no indications of anything about to happen. Christmas Eve came and with it, Edward's order that there was to be no drunkenness on Christmas Day. Following this announcement, certain adjutants of the 8th, 25th and 54th Foot confined their men to barracks, the 25th Foot even having their pay withheld.

It was certain irate wine-sellers who actually started the

trouble by smuggling brandy and wine to the 8th Foot. Inflamed with drink they broke out of their billets and marched on the 25th and 54th, inciting them to join in mutiny. When they refused, they were taunted as being cowards, and shots were fired.

Edward was furious that his evening's enjoyment had been interrupted, but on Julie's intervention, beyond threatening them with severe punishment should there be any further trouble, he let the matter drop.

The next day, however, the 25th, having now received their pay, went into town, stormed the wine shops and became roaring drunk. Now it was their turn to avenge the insults of Christmas Eve, when they had been dubbed cowards. Marching back to barracks they attacked the 8th Foot and in a fight that lasted three hours, three men were killed and several wounded.

Edward's rage was that of a madman. Again called away from his Christmas festivities, he it was who commanded the operation, ordering the shooting, and placing ten men, apparently the ring-leaders, under arrest, to be court-martialled the next day.

It was not Julie's custom to rise at the same early hour as Edward, but the next morning he was surprised to find her awaiting him in the breakfast-room.

He raised his eyebrows, frowning. 'What does this mean, Madame?'

'I wish to speak with you, Edward, before . . .'

'If it is to plead with me, you are wasting my time. I would enjoy my breakfast in silence, if you please.'

'Listen, Edward. Please be merciful. There can be no charge of a mutiny . . .'

'In the name of God, then what was it?'

'Nothing more than a brawl between drunken soldiers . . . It was Christmas Day, Edward. The men were seeking some kind of enjoyment . . . a little pleasure, crude as it was. What has Christmas meant for them . . . ?'

'Madame! I am not in the mood to listen to a sermon. I listened to you on Christmas Eve, and showed leniency. Now, even you must see that leniency in the army cannot be countenanced.'

She knew that he was in one of his deepest, black moods; knew that this was not the time to move him, yet she had to make one more attempt before those ten wretched men were brought before him.

'Sir. This is the season of goodwill towards all men. Please, please, Edward, do not sentence them to death.'

He pricked the yolk of his egg, so that it ran thickly over the gammon, and without lifting his eyes, remarked, 'That, Madame, is nothing more than silly sentimental woman talk . . .'

She knew that the men's fate was already settled.

    .   .   .   .   .

All ten men were sentenced to be shot, three of the sentences to be carried out immediately, the Duke calling out the whole garrison to watch the executions.

Lots were drawn from the 54th Foot to make up the firing squad. Taking up their position, they stood motionless, their faces inscrutable, but hating, as they had never hated before, hating the terrible duty ahead of them; hating the man who had ordered it. Without a sign of the rage in their hearts they saw their three former mess-mates marched across the barrack square, saw them line up in front; men who last night had drunk and cursed with them, before going off in search of a woman, and finding none, had come back reeling and staggering, seeking some other amusement.

'What about the bloody 8th? Called us cowards, they did, the bastards. Let's go and show them we're no bloody cowards.'

It had all begun as simple as that, and now ten men were to die an ignominious death. There was an eerie, tense silence over the barrack square. All men held their breath. Some silently prayed. Some silently cursed. A sharp, curt order split the air. Rifles were raised. Another order. The shots rang out and three bodies slumped to the ground.

As the corpses were carried off the troops re-formed and marched away, every man in step, holding his head at its correct angle, knowing that the hated Duke of Kent was watching, ready to pounce on any defaulter.

When Edward returned to the house, he found Julie writing notes to her friends, cancelling her assembly for that evening.

'But you must not do that, Julie. Cannot you see what it would mean?'

'I have no heart for entertaining; neither do I think our guests will have . . .'

'But it will appear that criticising my action . . . that you are taking the side of the others . . .'

'The others? Who?'

'Barnett . . . and certain other officers. I need your support, Julie, more now than ever . . . Please, Julie. After all, this is a military affair . . . military discipline . . . my work . . . The social life must go on as usual. Everyone will expect it. You'll see.'

Despite Edward's optimism and Julie's gift as a hostess, gloom settled over the Rock. Yet in one quarter there were sly winks as they raised their glasses. Was not this the beginning of the end of the Duke's reign as Governor?

By the next day, Edward had second thoughts as to his severity, commuting the other seven death sentences to transportation for life.

Until now he had sent regular reports back to Mr. Addington by every mail that left the Rock, but now he felt no written account of this latest débâcle could give a satisfactory explanation. Accordingly his aide-de-camp, Captain Thomas Dodd, was given the task of placing before the War Office the true facts in opposition to all the exaggerated stories he knew would emanate from the garrison. More-over, as Governor of Gibraltar, he demanded an enquiry into the behaviour of Major-General Barnett and other officers who, instead of assisting him, had contravened many of his orders.

Yet Edward already knew the outcome; knew that the Duke of York would gloatingly believe the worst. Now he knew the tortures of a condemned man waiting, hoping for a reprieve, the days between passing so slowly. He took to walking in the more secluded parts; anywhere to get away from his men . . . his officers . . . from the civilians.

It was during one of these rambles that he suddenly found the narrow path-way barred by a gypsy woman who stood regarding him as though lost in thought.

Edward tolerated her scrutiny for a moment or two and then, 'If you have no objection, my good woman, I would like to go my way.'

'You may as well listen to what I have to say, Your Royal Highness . . .'

'You know who I am then?'

She gave a brittle laugh. 'Who does not? The hated Duke of Kent? *I see many losses and crosses for you, Sir, but do not despair, you will die a happy man. You will have a daughter and she will become a great queen.*'

He delved into his pocket and offered her a coin. She made no move to take it, still subjecting him to a piercing look, before darting back into the bushes and shrubs.

Edward continued his walk, a cynical smile on his face. Daughter indeed. He wanted no daughter. He wanted no sons. Misery welled up again. Little did Julie know he regretted the lack of a family but as he saw it, his action was justified.

. . . . .

Thomas Dodd did not arrive back in Gibraltar until the

beginning of April, and it was bad news that he brought. By the King's command, His Royal Highness should return to England immediately. Edward was mortified, for the order went on to say that he should transfer his governorship to General Barnett who would take over until the newly appointed governor, General Trigge, arrived. Shame and ignominy overwhelmed him. That he, a royal duke, should be so disgraced before the whole garrison . . . and Barnett should go scot free . . . he who was supposed to uphold and support him.

Julie did her utmost to comfort him. 'Think, *mon chéri*, we shall enjoy all the comfort that your brothers take for granted. There will be time for your many other interests . . .'

'I am a soldier, Julie, a fighter, and I shall not let the matter rest. My actions must be vindicated . . .'

'Yes, Edward, yes,' she soothed.

When the time came for Edward and Julie to leave the Rock there was no dinner or dance this time. As became a fitting farewell to a King's son, General Barnett ordered a parade on the quay-side and as Edward walked between the ranks, he imagined he could see the scorn in every man's eye.

They were home by the end of May. Straightway, Edward wrote to the Home Secretary, Lord Pelham, asking to be court-martialled, so that he could justify all his actions. The letter and subsequent ones were ignored. A series of five letters to the Duke of York met with the same treatment until meeting his brother at the Queen's House he tackled him on the question. A violent argument ensued which, reaching the ears of the King, erased all the good feeling that had grown up between Edward and his father during the last few years.

As usual, Mrs. Fitzherbert's soothing company was sought. She was such a willing listener; the very fact of unburdening a troubled mind to her brought relief.

'And to think, Ma'am, before I even left the garrison, that rascal Barnett was already rescinding my orders; orders that were benefiting the troops; benefiting the civilians . . . and I am refused a hearing. Why, Ma'am, why?'

Maria eyed him steadily. 'I have always felt an affection for you, Sir, so I feel I can speak freely.'

'I should appreciate it, Ma'am, if you would.'

'I have listened to George and Frederick discoursing on the matter . . . and to others . . . and all are of the same opinion, that a court-martial would be fatal. The odds are that you would be found guilty, public opinion now being against excessively harsh or severe punishment . . . don't you see, Sir, no head of state would wish to put the King's son in such an invidious position.'

Edward was silent. What he had done, had been done in the name of duty. He had been asked to clean up Gibraltar.

'You are fortunate, Sir, in having such a loving companion as Madame de St. Laurent. You have your house at Castle Hill. I am so looking forward to seeing all the improvements you are making . . .'

So Edward threw himself into an orgy of lavish spending. Castle Hill should outshine Carlton House and the Pavilion. If, because he was a king's son, he could not have a fair hearing, then, by Heavens, he would live like a king's son.

7

Edward now had four establishments to maintain: the house in Knightsbridge; his official apartments in Kensington Palace; Castle Hill Lodge and the Pavilion at Hampton Court, where he had been appointed Ranger of the Park.

It was at Castle Hill that Edward and Julie lived most of their time; where they did most of their entertaining. He had already spent over £100,000 on reconstruction and decorating, incorporating many odd, expensive ideas. When Julie attempted to remonstrate concerning the exorbitant costs, she was immediately silenced. His expenses were nowhere near those of his brothers.

It was his library that was his great pride and joy, a huge, square room on the ground floor, lined with shelves from floor to ceiling, shelves that he intended to fill with the choicest books from all the eminent writers, past and contemporary.

Madame, too, was fond of reading, but her books must not intermingle with his, so she had her own library on the floor above.

When it came to selecting his household, he had been quick to remember the kindness of Major-General Vilette appointing him as his comptroller. Captain Dodd, of course, maintained his post as chief secretary; then came grooms of the chamber, equerries, physicians, surgeons, apothecaries, even a surgeon-dentist, and thirteen chaplains!

Soothed by the joint efforts of Julie and Mrs. Fitzherbert, Edward attempted to find other outlets for his energy, giving his patronage to various charities and organisations.

Mrs. Fitzherbert had presented Julie to Princess Caroline, but now that Maria was reunited with George, she rarely visited the Princess herself, knowing it was against her husband's wishes. This, however, did not deter Edward and Julie from accepting invitations, for, like the other royal dukes, they had much sympathy for the unhappy lady. Admittedly, she did act in an odd and foolish manner, but wasn't that due to George's cruel behaviour?

It was at one of her assemblies that she approached Edward and Julie, apparently in one of her silly, play-acting moods.

'Ah, my dear, dear cousin Edward. The very man I am searching for.' She looked archly at Julie. 'Will you have any strong objections, Madame, if I take him away from you for a few minutes, just long enough to . . .' She allowed her voice to trail away, at the same time ogling Edward with a sly, almost lewd grimace.

Julie laughed gently, 'I am not the Duke's keeper.'

'Then come, *mon amour*, where none shall disturb us . . .'

Edward attempted to shake her off his arm, which she had taken possessively.

'What is all this about, Princess?' he asked irritably.

In answer she took a firmer grip and led him to the library. Inside, he shook himself free, squaring his shoulders. 'Now, Your Highness, an explanation.'

She made a childish moue. 'I thought you were the one I could turn to for help.'

'Help? What kind of help?'

She came nearer to him, whispering, 'To get rid of some undesirable detestable people.'

Edward laughed with relief. 'Well, if that is all . . . who are they?'

'Sir John and Lady Douglas.'

Edward frowned, thinking back. 'But are they not dear friends of yours? Have I not met them in this very house?'

'They are no longer my friends. I have discovered that Lady Douglas has on several occasions betrayed my confidence. Now I do not wish to see her, yet she continues to call, though my servants have orders not to admit her. So she sends notes . . . rude notes . . .'

'. . . and you wish me to see Sir John to ask him and his wife to cease pestering you?'

'Oh, Cousin Edward, if you would, please,' and to Edward's consternation, he found Caroline's plump arms around his neck, and kisses being rained upon his cheeks.

Edward felt the perspiration on his forehead. Heavens, if anybody was to open the door, they would immediately think the worst.

Disengaging himself and mopping his forehead, he said coolly, 'Had you not better be getting back to your guests?'

'Indeed, yes. Your delightful Madame Julie will be thinking I have seduced you . . .'

Edward's mouth set in a hard line. Silly, foolish woman. No wonder she had trouble with her so-called friends.

Julie showed much concern as she listened to Edward's story of the interview. 'I do not like it, Edward. Remember the last time you helped her? There was trouble with your brother.'

'I have no intention of telling George. The less he hears of her foolish squabbles the better. I'll placate this Sir John, but why men should be called upon to settle women's squabbles, I don't know.'

    •   •   •   •   •

It was a very agitated Edward who, having bade good morning to his caller, Sir John Douglas, raced upstairs to Julie's room.

She looked up from her desk as he entered. '*Mon Dieu*,

Edward, you are in a fine tizzy. What has now displeased you?'

'That woman! That foolish, stupid, imbecile my cousin, the Princess of Wales. Little wonder my brother had no patience with her ...'

'Suppose you tell me her latest offence ...'

' 'Tis the Douglas affair. I asked Sir John to call, to inform him he must cease pestering Her Highness; to tell him she had tired of the friendship with his wife ...' He paused, being uncertain of his next words.

'Well ... ?'

' 'Tis not they who are being offensive ... 'tis the Princess ... depraved ... disgustingly so ...' Edward was almost shouting; his voice full of anger.

'You still do not tell me ...'

'It is not fit to tell you ... or any other decent woman.' Julie made no insistence. He would tell her when he was ready. She had not long to wait. Having found control of his voice and anger, he said slowly, 'The Princess had sent to Sir John the most vulgar, lewd drawing that anyone could conceive, depicting Lady Douglas in the arms of Sir Philip Sydney, a mutual friend of them both.'

'I do not believe it! She may be silly ... even vulgar ... but surely not ...'

'That was my retort, until Sir John showed me the drawing. There was writing on the paper ... more vulgar indecencies and I recognised the handwriting ...'

'Poor, poor Edward. How could she put you into such a terrible position, to ask you to mediate for her? Were you able to conciliate Sir John?'

'I almost went down on my knees to the fellow. Begged of him that the matter should go no further. Pleaded the case for the King's health. Pleaded for Caroline, pointing out the scandal if the Prince of Wales should hear of the matter ...'

'And were you successful?'

'I think so . . . but of Lady Douglas I am not so sure. Apart from the wicked untruth, she considers herself most seriously injured . . .'

'And quite rightly so, Sir. A woman can betray her husband, and enjoy the experience, but when it is untrue . . . *Mon Dieu* . . . it is both injury and insult! Now Sir, cease pestering yourself. You have performed the service she asked. You and Sir John have parted amicably . . .'

'Just pray God the Prince of Wales does not hear of it.'

. . . . .

Edward was feeling pleased with life. George had written requesting that the Duke of Kent should call on him at Carlton House. Invitations from the Prince of Wales had been very sparse since the trouble over Princess Caroline's household accounts. Not that he blamed his brother; the trouble was that he was too easily influenced by the Duke of York. Indeed, his heart had warmed to George when on a recent occasion they had been in the company of Mr. Addington, the ex-Prime Minister. The three of them had paced the room together, George with his arm around Edward's shoulders, discussing the Gibraltar affair, and finally observing :

'You send a man out to control a garrison all but in open mutiny. You tell him to terminate such a disgraceful state and assure him of the government's unqualified support. He goes out and finds things infinitely worse than stated. The impending outbreak occurs. He quells it thoroughly. By way of reward you disgrace him. If you want to deter an officer from his duty or encourage a mutinous soldier your tactics are admirable. Edward may well complain. He were neither an officer nor a man if he were silent.'

He knew then that the Duke of York was his worse enemy, not George.

Arriving at Carlton House he was surprised to see the

Duke of Sussex' coach being driven round to the stables. So he was not the only guest. George must be holding some kind of celebration.

When he entered the library, neither George nor his brother the Duke of Sussex gave him any kind of welcome save for perfunctory nods, and an indication to be seated.

George lost no time in coming to the point.

'You know of a certain Sir John Douglas?'

'Why, yes . . .'

'And some time last year, you asked him to call on you.'

'Yes.'

'To discuss a personal affair concerning his wife's honour and the Princess of Wales?'

'Yes. The Princess asked me . . .'

'Since when has it been your prerogative to attend the Princess' behests . . . ?'

'Sir. I am becoming weary of this cross-examination, as though I was prisoner at the bar.' He could not control the anger in his voice. 'The Princess sought my aid, and as a gentleman I could not refuse it.'

'But you will admit, will you not, brother, that you discovered more than you bargained for? Why did you not report your findings to me?'

'For the most obvious of reasons. Concern for the King's health and to avoid a scandal.'

'Scandal! Bah! King's health! Poppy-cock! Are you not aware that Sir John is now in the service of the Duke of Sussex?'

'I am.'

'And has the knowledge never caused you any qualms?'

'Why should it? I had Sir John's word that he would let the matter drop . . . Obviously he has now spoken of it.'

'With all good reason, for the Princess, far from dropping the matter, has on every possible occasion taunted and tormented Lady Douglas, so that in the end her husband felt compelled to report the matter to our brother.'

'. . . and our brother felt compelled to report the matter to you.' There was contempt in every word that Edward uttered.

George's fist came banging down on the table. 'He is loyal to the family . . . no hiding family matters away. Do you know what you have done? By deliberately keeping back this information you have prevented my application for divorce; to be rid of this . . . this woman. But it's not too late! There was other information, wasn't there? What about her illegitimate child . . . Wilkins?'

Edward had to laugh at the stupidity of the name. 'Oh yes I've heard of him . . . met him in fact. He's not her child . . .'

'She told Lady Douglas herself . . .'

'Maybe. I gather that is the way the ladies often talked to each other . . . pure nonsense . . .'

'The whole business is to be investigated . . . the King is to be told . . . and no interference on your part can prevent it. The Princess has behaved in a scandalous manner . . . and you, Sir, have aided and abetted her.'

There was nothing Edward could say to enable his brother to see the truth; George wanted a divorce, therefore Caroline had to be proved guilty. Now he realised he was more out of favour with his brother than ever before.

Julie was shocked at this new turn. 'Every time you try to help Caroline, your actions are misconstrued . . .'

'But never again. Never again will I go to her assistance. There is something unfortunate about her that rubs off on to me . . .'

. . . . . .

The investigation was held. Edward was called to give evidence but refused to be drawn into it although he was fully convinced the lewd drawing was Caroline's handiwork. In gratitude the Princess wrote to the King : *Being impressed with the belief of Lady Douglas' story that I was the author of the drawing, he did that which naturally became him under such belief; he endeavoured, for the peace of Your Majesty and the honour of the Royal Family, to keep from the knowledge of the world what. if it had been true, would have justly reflected such infinite disgrace on me.'*

To her husband's chagrin, she was found to be innocent of adultery, and the investigations came to an end, Edward still reiterating, 'Never again.'

* * * * *

All was hustle and bustle at Castle Hill, so much coming and going; so much chattering and laughter along the softly carpeted corridors. Even the flunkeys in their immaculate uniforms, complete with white gloves, relaxed their usual composed faces, to allow an occasional grin, when a young voice would query, 'Say, Uncle Edward, how does this dancing bear work?' Or, 'My, Aunt Julie, you look mighty fine in that dress!'

Three of the de Salaberry boys had descended upon them, the eldest, Charles, now an army captain in London for three months, and Maurice and Chevalier, still cadets, on their way to Scotland to join their regiment.

Julie was in raptures. Their visit was such a joyous break in their more-or-less humdrum life. When they had been announced, Charles had taken her in his arms and swung her off her feet, flattering her that she didn't look a day older than when she had left Canada ten years ago. She almost wept as she kissed the two younger boys; they had been so small when she last saw them. Edward found Charles a delightful companion, giving him rooms in Kensington Palace, but dining each day with him and Julie either at Knightsbridge or Castle Hill . . . and what an excellent officer! Within two months he had recruited a hundred and fifty men for the Royals!

When she wrote to Catherine de Salaberry she couldn't extol the boys' virtues enough. So good looking! Such charming manners! All she and the Duke were now waiting for was the arrival next year of their godson, Edward, who would be fourteen and entering, on Edward's recommendation, Woolwich Military Training College.

. . . . .

When the investigation failed to find Caroline guilty, she was vastly relieved, but at the same time full of jubilation at the downfall of her tormentors.

She was aware that news of the trial would have filtered through to Germany, and therefore set about writing her relatives her account of the story. Her elation was such that she could not resist deriding her in-laws; her imbecile father-in-law; the ugly little Queen; the Princesses, married and unmarried; the royal dukes and their mistresses; all came under the lash of her pen. She dare not send the letters by the royal couriers; George was probably already opening her correspondence, so she looked around and found a clergyman about to visit Germany. All arrangements were made, and the package of letters put in his care. Then, at the last moment, he had a change of plan, and accordingly sent back the packet of letters to Caroline. No more was heard of them until a very angry queen sent for the Princess. The letters had come into her hands. Caroline had no excuse. The cruel, bitter, sarcastic words, humiliating all concerned, was only matched by her own self-inflicted humiliation. The letters were bundled up and sent to George, so that he should know the small, belittling mind of his wife. George passed them on to the Duke of York; then to all the other brothers.

Remembering his vow of 'Never again', Edward refused to read them, sending them back to George with a note: *'They were unjustifiable letters which it was hardly possible* to reconcile with the rank of the writer. I have not seen the letters for various reasons, among them being a conviction that their being in existence at all . . . was a breach of that honourable confidence which ought to actuate all persons in matters where private correspondence is concerned.'

George's anger knew no bounds. The sanctimonious prig! So he wouldn't read anyone else's correspondence? So again he was aiding and abetting that vile woman; encouraging her to write such scurrilous outpourings against the Royal Family! The less he saw of Edward the better.

Both Edward and Julie felt the injustice keenly, especially as Edward had been about to seek George's aid in recovering money for the loss of seven equipments. Now, for several months at least, there would be no invitations to Carlton House or the Pavilion. No use invoking Maria's aid, for the knowledge had become common that the Prince had taken another mistress—Lady Hertford.

.   .   .   .   .

Throughout the early months of 1806, Julie gave much thought to the impending visit of their godson. As he was only fourteen, she and Edward had agreed to be responsible for him while in England and though the prospect filled her with joy, yet deep down she wondered whether she would find his continued presence too emotional, for the short stay of his three brothers had vaguely disturbed her. Yet when he arrived, she could not contain her excitement. Edward was everything she would have wished for in her own son; boyishly handsome, so lovable in that he was young enough to respond to Julie's kisses and embraces. He stood in no awe of the Duke: indeed he treated him with the same respectful casualness as he did his own papa.

Naturally he was engrossed with all the mechanical devices about the house; a veritable toyshop for a boy.

Julie and Edward were determined that his stay with

them should have nothing but happy memories. There were visits to the theatre, having all London asking as to the identity of the handsome boy seen so frequently in the Duke of Kent's box.

There were happy evenings at home, playing draughts and dominoes, Edward and Julie always being beaten. Watching young Edward planning a crafty move, Julie would think, 'This is how family life should be. Within the home. This is how it could have been for us.' Then she would give herself a mental shake and smile at the disappearance of three kings in one fell swoop.

There were days when she liked to pretend he was her own son, taking him shopping, buying him clothes and gifts and giving him pocket-money. Though she knew his parents were missing him sorely—their youngest child—she told herself that while it might be very selfish, she was glad he would probably be with them for a considerable time.

Charles was now in Ireland but coming to spend Christmas with them. Christmas still held the thrill of magic for her and this year was going to be more festive than ever. Her daily life was now so full she had no time for dwelling on 'what might have been'. She accepted the present with all thankfulness.

There were other guests for Christmas — the Duc d'Orléans and his two brothers. Since their return to Europe, a strong friendship had developed between them and the Duke. Not only was Louis a frequent visitor at Castle Hill but Edward had had a bedroom in Kensington Palace put at his constant disposal.

Castle Hill rang with merriment that year, young Edward enjoying the company of grown-ups for the first time in his life; grown-ups who enjoyed the company of young people, English, French and Canadians enjoying a truly traditional English Christmas. Since she had met Edward, Christmas had been a very, very special event in her life.

Dearest Papa,

I am at present staying with H.R.H. the Duke of Kent at Kensington Palace, where I have fine apartments. H.R.H. and Madame de St. Laurent are at Knightsbridge, which is some distance from here. It is a superb mansion, beautifully furnished. I dined there on Christmas Day with the Duke of Orléans and his brothers. I have been at the Opera with H.R.H. and Madame, when I saw the Duke of Cambridge to whom I was presented . . . I have also seen the Swedish Ambassador . . . H.R.H. has given orders that we shall always have music at dinner. The Duke and Madame have been very kind to me . . . My letters cost me nothing . . . they all come first to H.R.H. and then to me; the postage is paid at the Palace. Adieu, my dear Papa. I believe I shall see you before long, and I am with the most lively affection,

Your devoted and obedient son
Edward Alphonse de S.

P.S. Madame has given me six guineas since I came to England, a jolly sum for me.

P.P.S. Aunt Julie is very insistent that I clean my teeth each day. She says 'there is a kind of little worm in the teeth, that you can't see with your eyes, but that they are like toads and that if you don't brush your teeth like you should, they will gradually eat them away'.

.   .   .   .   .

The morning air was fragrant with summer flowers and as Julie and Edward strolled through the gardens of Castle Hill, Edward laconically remarked, 'My mother, Her Majesty the Queen, has expressed a wish to visit Castle Hill . . . my sisters, too, Mary and Elizabeth, for they are ever enquiring about you. Have you any preference as to when the visit should take place?'

Julie continued to snip off fallen roses, conscious that she was breathing hard.

'I leave it to you, Sir . . . any day . . . the gardens are now at their best . . . but . . . but what does this portend? Why Her Majesty's sudden interest?'

'Sheer curiosity, *ma petite*. I have talked much of the house. My brothers have told of certain unusual characteristics. Isn't it a commonplace practice for one woman to want to look over another's newly acquired home?'

An uneasy feeling was seeping into her mind.

'It is the house . . . only the house she . . . Her Majesty wishes to see?'

'And the gardens of course . . . and I shall entertain them to lunch and dinner.'

'What I meant, Sir . . . she is now desirous of meeting me?'

He hesitated. 'Not exactly, my darling. While you will make all arrangements . . . I . . . I hate to tell you that you cannot be by my side . . . to meet her.'

'No? Then who?'

'There lies a problem. The Queen will not meet the Princess of Wales . . . the Duchess of York is separated from the Duke . . . Nevertheless, I will have to ask her to do the honours.'

Noticing her crestfallen appearance, he took her hand. 'Why does it upset you, Julie? You have never protested concerning your lack of invitation to Court.'

'No . . . but . . . not to be hostess in my own . . . in your house . . .'

' 'Tis but a matter of protocol, my sweet . . .'

. . . . . .

The Duchess of York was only too pleased to come out of

her seclusion. Taking care to be as unobtrusive as possible, Julie made deep obeisance as the Queen and the Princesses entered the vast hall with its marble floor and pillars, giving a sigh of relief when Edward led the Queen's party on a tour of the house.

She could imagine their exclamations of surprise first in this room and then that; at the enormous collection of clocks and mechanical devices. Would he show them the new-fangled water-closets attached to the main bedrooms?

At lunch-time, she arranged to be seated with the ladies-in-waiting, but even with them, she felt unusually ill at ease, for though they made polite conversation, their condescension was obvious.

When the party went into the garden she would have preferred to stay indoors but Edward came searching her out.

'Come. I wish to present you to my sisters. Mama is driving round the pleasure gardens.'

The Princesses made no secret of their delight in meeting her. 'Madame de St. Laurent, we hear of you every time Edward visits us . . . and . . . and we are so grateful to you for your great care of our brother.'

It was easy after that; easy to accept the heavily painted Duchess with the blinking eyes and chattering tongue sitting in her place by Edward's side; easy to tolerate the Queen's rigidity, stifling a smile each time the little lady took a pinch of snuff.

When the last carriage had disappeared down the long, winding drive, Edward placed a loving arm around her. 'Not such a terrible ordeal was it my love?'

'Anything I do for you, Sir, is always a pleasure,' she answered quietly.

.   .   .   .   .

Throughout the months that followed, Julie had little time

for repining. Young Edward with them whenever he was free from college; their visits to him, to mark his progress; odd visits from Maurice and Chevalier until their final leave before embarking for India. Feverishly she threw herself into organising a series of entertainments for them, but all too soon came the moment of parting. Then, while the Duke drove them down to Portsmouth, she sat down to write to their mother, dear, dear Souris, assuring her of the wonderful prospects of serving in India.

'I hope they will find the country healthy and have rapid promotion in their service . . . If one is convinced that the country is good for speculators it must be advantageous to others and all officers on that account strive to get the preference to accompany troops to India.'

.   .   .   .   .

From the beginning of their association, Edward had insisted on giving Julie a regular allowance and she, being of a thrifty nature, had over the years built up considerable savings, so once they were established in England, she sought the advice of Mr. Coutts as to investment. Edward was all in favour as he had always felt some definite provision should be made for his dear Madame should he predecease her.

She still had the well-being of her family at heart, especially that of her youngest brother, Jean-Claude, who when financially embarrassed frequently applied to his sister, who willingly went to his aid. Now she wished to put the help on a more permanent basis, arranging, with Mr. Coutts' valuable assistance, regular quarterly payments. Again, Edward offered no objection, taking a keen interest in Julie's young nephews and nieces.

8

The news from Gibraltar was most alarming. The rumour was rapidly gaining ground that Joseph Bonaparte, King of Spain, was planning to recapture the garrison.

Edward was still governor of Gibraltar; still receiving his annual pay of £3,500, having neither resigned nor been dismissed. He was the only man, he brooded, who could save the Rock; he being an experienced soldier.

Accordingly, he wrote his father, *'begging leave to impress upon Your Majesty's attention everything most dear to me in life; my character; my professional credit as a soldier are at stake.'*

Daily, he expected a call to the Queen's House to be given permission to return to the garrison, but as the weeks passed without any reply, he realised the futility of his hopes. Then came a cruel, scathing letter from his brother, the Duke of York, practically demanding his resignation. Angrily, Edward appealed to the government, but again his pleas for active service were rejected.

The inertia irked him. He was depressed and moody; difficult to live with, severely taxing and straining Julie's usual placid outlook.

'. . . but Sir, you are doing much good work for the people . . . be content . . .'

'I am a soldier . . . I am but turned forty years of age . . . and here I sit . . . day after day . . .'

'Yet have you not often said, *mon chéri*, that so long as we had each other . . .'

'A man needs two lives . . . a public life and a private life
. . . the one to complement the other. Either on its own is
apt to become stale . . . *passé* . . .'

Julie felt a premonition of fear. Was Edward tiring of
her? A premonition of Maria Fitzherbert's fate passed
through her mind . . . and there were the rumours that the
Duke of Clarence was dancing attendance on other ladies.

If Edward did return to Gibraltar, and there was real
danger of attack, she would be left behind in England.
Would that be such a bad thing? He would send for her as
soon as the danger was over, and she would find him like
the lover of old, strengthened and re-vitalised. Yet the
thought of being parted made her so wretched and miserable that though she realised her selfishness, she could not
altogether share his disappointment.

He was now connected with fifty-three different organisations; charitable, educational and recreational. To them
he was the very epitome of a perfect prince; kindly,
courteous and generous; subscribing liberally to their funds,
despite his own heavy debts, and most certainly much
maligned over the Gibraltar affair.

It was his secretary, Dodd, recently promoted major, who
drew his attention to a pamphlet that had arrived with
the mail. Edward stared at the outer cover with its bold
title, '*Observations on His Royal Highness the Duke of
Kent's Shameful Persecution, Since his Recall from Gibraltar.*'

He scanned the pages with growing bewilderment . . .
fawning adulation for himself . . . criticism of the Duke of
York . . . a suggestion that the Duke of Kent should replace
him as Commander-in-Chief . . . With him in command,
the war in Portugal would be quickly ended . . . and still
more insults that the Duke of York would be better employed as a Prussian drill-sergeant . . . or a tailor.

'Who in the name of Hell is the author of this trash?'
he demanded.

Major Dodd shrugged his shoulders. 'I have no notion, Sir . . . but obviously an admirer . . . or perhaps a group of well-wishers.'

'Then I would thank them to keep their opinions to themselves. Whatever differences there are between the Commander-in-Chief and myself is our private affair. Imagine my brother's feelings . . . and rage . . . when he reads this.'

'. . . and yet, Sir, may I take this opportunity to say that I endorse their sentiments. You would make a better Commander-in-Chief, and you . . .'

'Enough. I thank you for your loyalty, but it is dangerous talk. Let it go no further. Instead . . . do your utmost to trace the writer of this—this rubbish.'

Julie was equally disturbed when she read the pamphlet.

'Well-wishers,' she scoffed. 'Mischief-makers would be more correct. You must contact the Duke of York at once and persuade him of your ignorance.'

'Too late . . . he will already have had the matter brought to his notice. Already he'll be howling imprecations at my very existence . . .'

'Yet you must go and clear yourself . . .'

As he expected, Frederick was in a towering rage, hurling accusation after accusation upon him, until finally, tired of hearing Edward's denials, he shouted, 'Then it must be Dodd, that damned secretary of yours . . .'

'Ridiculous. The man is devoted to me . . .'

'Exactly. So devoted that he would turn to any trick to advance your cause . . . to win the sympathy of the people. He is an ambitious man, is Major Dodd. Do you think he enjoys toying with the correspondence of this hospital . . . that musical society? No, Sir, no. He's got his sights set on being secretary to the Commander-in-Chief . . . so he supplies the information of all the cruel injustices heaped upon you . . .'

'Enough, Sir. I tell you Dodd is incapable of such deceit ...'

'Then find out who is the originator of this filth ... but in the meantime, keep out of my sight ...'

'Too gladly, for let me say, now I know you are the cause of all my misfortunes ...'

Julie was all tact and sympathy, but she could see that the quarrel had gone deep. 'You know, Sir, your brother has recently separated from Mrs. Clarke. Perhaps the disruption has unsettled him and made him over-wrought.'

'On the contrary. I heard it from his own lips some weeks ago that he was overjoyed to be rid of her, she being so avaricious and grasping.'

'Then perhaps he is lonely ...'

'*Ma petite*, you would attempt an excuse for the Devil himself, for already Frederick has found consolation in the arms of a certain Mrs. Carey.'

Julie fell silent. Again she felt that barb of fear. How quickly these royal brothers, save her beloved Edward, discarded their mistresses, without any sign of remorse. She felt impelled to ask, 'Your brother, William, is it true he is contemplating ... marriage?'

'Gossip. Gossip. Gossip. True he is spending much time with Miss Tylney-Long ... true, she is an heiress ... true, my brother is in the same boat as the rest of us—up to his ears in debt, but what lady in her right senses will take on a family of ten bastard children?'

She winced. 'But of Mrs. Jordan? After all these years ... with such a large family ... some still young children ... what would become of them?'

'They were foolish in the first place, to embarrass themselves with a family. Now if there is to be a parting, they must face up to the consequences.'

'Mrs. Clarke ... I hear she has left her house in Gloucester Place ...'

'So I believe ... and returned from whence she came ...

to nowhere. Thank God you and Maria Fitzherbert refused to meet her, a woman of low morals and no breeding. I deplore my brother's taste.'

Now barred from Carlton House and the Pavilion, life became tedious for both himself and Julie. How glad they were of their friendship with Maria Fitzherbert . . . and Thomas Coutts, for a warm friendship had emerged through their business relationship, he being made cognisant of all their private affairs.

· · · · ·

Towards the end of the year, Edward became ill and despite all Julie's ministrations, made but slow recovery. It had begun with an ordinary cold, which he chose to ignore, refusing to call the doctor, although his household boasted several—knowing that their initial treatment would be to bleed him, a treatment in which he had little faith. Both he and Julie were accustomed to having colds each winter, blaming the change from sunny Gibraltar to the ice and snow of Canada, but down the years they had learned to comfort and sympathise with each other, Julie becoming wise in her treatment of sneezes and wheezes.

Dusk was rapidly closing in on a late January afternoon when Major Dodd was announced. Edward looked up in surprise for he and his secretary had spent the whole morning dealing with correspondence. Something of importance must have cropped up. Major Dodd glanced across from the Duke to Madame de St. Laurent. Julie was quick to catch the look.

'I will leave you, gentlemen, to your conversation . . .'

'No, Madame. I would prefer you stayed. You can speak freely, Dodd, before Madame de St. Laurent. She and I have no secrets.'

'Sir, this afternoon, a certain Colonel Wardle rose in the House of Commons to ask that a committee be formed to enquire into the conduct of His Royal Highness, the Duke of York.'

A look of incredulity passed over Edward's face, while Julie stared in bewilderment at first one gentleman and then the other.

'Conduct of His Royal Highness? A committee? An enquiry?' Edward's astonishment came blurting out. 'What are you talking about? Who is this Colonel Wardle?'

'He is the Member of Parliament for Okehampton, Sir. A Whig. Apparently he has discovered that a certain friend of His Highness . . . a lady friend, has, under his direction, been selling commissions for her own and the Duke's pocket . . .'

'Nonsense. Infamous. I have no love for my brother, but he would never stoop so low. Who is the . . . the so-called lady?'

'Mrs. Clarke . . .'

It was rare that Edward used violent language in Julie's presence, but now he used every invective that came to his tongue, to denounce his brother's former mistress. 'Isn't it obvious, that such a story could only come from a cheap, loud mouthed whore of her standing?'

'But, Sir, there is the word of the officers who paid Mrs. Clarke . . . £2,000 for a majority, £1,500 for a captaincy, £550 for a lieutenancy, and £400 for an ensign.'

'My God, no wonder she lived in such opulent style. On the one hand she was always moaning that my brother gave her but a poor allowance, yet she could afford to take a house at Gloucester Place, staff it complete with maids and footmen, butler and chef . . . keep two carriages and eight horses in her stable . . .'

'Exactly, Sir, but the enquiry is to ascertain the Duke's part in the business . . .'

'I've already told you. Dodd. My brother would have no part in it . . . but a public enquiry . . . to have all his private affairs exposed . . . Why? How did it come about?'

143

'Mrs. Clarke feels herself a very ill-used woman, Sir, since His Highness broke off their acquaintance last year. She is willing to talk.'

'So she is out to ruin my brother? What does she expect to gain?'

Major Dodd shrugged his shoulders. 'Self satisfaction, I suppose Sir . . . Revenge.'

.   .   .   .   .

The enquiry, held at the bar of the House of Commons, had begun, the press and the public alike enjoying the candid revelations of a royal mistress.

Mrs. Clarke was also enjoying herself; recalling amorous incidents; reading the absurd, sentimental letters that had passed between them; revealing intimate details of the Duke's frailties and failings, holding him up as a figure of fun for all to deride.

Edward, still housebound, and relying for reports of the enquiry from friends and the news-sheets, was horrified, not only at the revelations, but that a woman could so use the man who had been her lover. Time and again, he would take Julie's hand in his, perhaps when passing or crossing the room, to murmur, 'Thank God we are not as they,' but when reports mentioned the name of Captain Dodd as being implicated with Colonel Wardle, he heard the ominous, rumbling thunder. Then the thunderbolt. He, Edward, Duke of Kent was cited as being the man behind Colonel Wardle, in his scheme to dishonour his brother, the Duke of York.

'Tomorrow, I go to the House of Lords. I will not have this vile lie held against me.' His voice was cold and hard.

'But you are not well enough to go out in this treacherous February weather . . .' protested Julie.

'No weather, however bitter, could be so treacherous as certain scoundrels. Have no fear, *ma petite*, I will guard myself well against all.'

There was a buzz of suppressed excitement when he took his seat in the House. What had he come to tell them, to explain? There were many who were disappointed at the lack of fireworks; Edward simply stating that while he and the Duke of York had several personal and professional differences, he had such trust and confidence in his brother to know him to be incapable of such behaviour as accused by Mrs. Clarke.

It was a matter of conjecture as to whether his statement to the Lords swayed the Commons, but at the closing of the enquiry, the House voted its confidence in the Commander-in-Chief by a majority of eighty-two.

Frederick, however, was not satisfied. That one hundred and ninety-six members could believe him guilty went against his pride. He immediately resigned his post.

.   .   .   .   .

Mrs. Fitzherbert had called for tea, and the ladies, in the absence of Edward, were enjoying an uninhibited session of gossip. Despite that Maria and George were again more or less parted, she was still considered to be London's leading hostess and Queen of Brighton. Hence all gossip reached Maria. They spoke of the vile Mrs. Clarke, wondering where she had gone to earth; they sympathised with the poor Duchess of York, living with her dogs and cats and monkeys; they pondered as to the possible fate of Dorothy Jordan . . . and would William dare propose to Miss Tylney-Long?

She was full of chatter about her twelve-year-old Minney, her adopted daughter—her beauty—her charm. Julie listened in silence. Dear God, for the companionship of a child. How long would it be before the de Salaberry boys came a-visiting again? She was recalled from her day-dream by Maria's continuous chatter—the ridiculous behaviour of the Prince of Wales—George's fiendish treatment of both her and the Princess.

Mrs. Clarke had been a very busy woman. She had need to be, for her finances were in a very low state. She had written a book entitled *The Rival Princes*, dealing with the lives of the Duke of York and the Duke of Kent. Apart from material she was already familiar with, having been Frederick's mistress for six years, she had gone around gleaning and acquiring tit-bits of gossip concerning Edward and Julie.

The theme of her book was that Edward was responsible for the Duke of York's fall. Edward, she claimed, had offered her, through Dodd, five thousand pounds and four hundred a year, if she would give evidence that would discountenance the Duke of York. Not only did she poke fun at the two brothers, but Julie also came under the scourge of her pen. Perhaps Mrs. Clarke was taking her revenge for Julie's previous 'nose-in-the-air' attitude towards her, but whatever it was, both Edward and Julie were revolted by the wicked calumniations of *The Rival Princes* and the realisation that it was enjoying a lucrative sale to rich and poor alike.

Edward was almost speechless when he first read the accusations.

'Why?' he stormed. 'Why have I to be embroiled in my brother's amorous affairs? Why, because he discards a worthless mistress, have I to have false accusations heaped upon me?'

Julie wept bitterly. There were several hurtful taunts levelled at her. *'Edward's old French lady'* had been Mrs. Clarke's name for her, but she dried her eyes to comfort Edward, who was still raging.

'I was friendly towards the Princess of Wales, and gave her my assistance . . . and to what end? I incurred the anger of my brother. I avoided Mrs. Clarke with the same result. My second brother took it as an insult that I ignored her and refused to present you to her. In the name of God, what am I to do? Tell me, Julie. Tell me.'

Her answer was slow in coming, then, 'There is only one man who can prove you were not behind Colonel Wardle . . .'

'You mean the man himself? Never. I want no dealings with a scoundrel who could initiate such a scandal . . .'

'No . . . not Colonel Wardle . . . Major Dodd.'

'You do not think . . .'

'He is the only man who can refute Mrs. Clarke's statement that you offered her, through him, that vast amount of money . . .'

'You are right, Julie. You are right. But how can it be done, without another enquiry which, if I demanded it, would most probably be refused?'

'We must think this out very carefully, *mon ami*. Could you not get signed statements to the contrary from Major Dodd?'

Between them Edward and Julie drew up a series of written questions directed at Major Dodd: Had the Duke of Kent ever advised an attack on the Duke of York? Had the Major ever heard him express a wish to see his brother disgraced? Had he ever known Edward to have any dealings with Colonel Wardle or Mrs. Clarke? Had he ever heard him express the wish to be Commander-in-Chief?

To all these questions and several others, Major Dodd replied in the negative, signing each question separately. Only then did Edward send out copies to his brothers, the Prince of Wales and the Duke of York, and much to Edward's and Julie's gratification, the Duke of York appeared to be somewhat conciliated.

It was obvious, however, that Major Dodd had played no small part in the scandal, and immediately after signing the statements, resigned his post. Now that the cloud was lifted, Edward could afford to be generous, writing to the Duke of Orléans that Major Dodd's resignation was '*a necessary sacrifice to public opinion*,' adding that he was '*more to be pitied than blamed in many things and the imprudent things which he has unfortunately done have come from too great an enthusiasm for my service and too lively a sense of all the injustices we have suffered.'*

.   .   .   .   .

London was in a festive mood, for it was celebrating His Majesty's fifty years upon the throne of England. There were balls and assemblies at all the great houses, where ladies in velvets and silks trod a stately measure with elegantly dressed, powdered and perfumed gentlemen. There were banquets of eighteen or twenty courses, banquets which went on unceasingly, guests falling asleep, ready to begin again on awakening. Up and down the land, town and country alike, the masses came out of their hovels to participate in the free meals provided by the parish—even a taste of the roasted ox, if they were lucky enough; to gape at the fireworks and call three cheers for His Majesty . . . a majesty who was indifferent to it all; blind, dim-witted and frail. Within the royal circle, there was a better atmosphere blowing through the salons of the Prince of Wales, Frederick and Edward; Edward entertaining his brothers at Castle Hill Lodge; and in turn he and Julie being welcomed back to Carlton House.

.   .   .   .   .

Sorrow was swift to follow upon jubilation. Princess Amelia, Their Majesties' youngest daughter, was dead. She had suffered from the wasting disease for a number of years, and all had known she had not long to live, yet the blow was still severe. She was the pet of her brothers and sisters alike, and the very delight of her ageing, ailing father. With her death, the last thread holding together the King's sanity snapped. Edward and his brothers were all together discussing the inevitable outcome of their father's latest

143

break-down. The Regency could not now be long delayed. George was excited and voluble; full of plans, indifferent that they were gathered to solemnise a funeral of a much loved sister. The Queen pressed them to stay on; not only had she the sorrow of losing her daughter but the burden of an imbecile husband. The funeral over, however, Edward had only one desire, to get back to the peace of Castle Hill Lodge.

. . . . .

The Regency had been declared. There was riotous jubilation at Carlton House, as hangers-on called on George with their congratulations, all hoping for a share in the good times to come.

There must be a ball; a ball to outshine all others, but it could hardly be known as the Regency Ball, for that would be celebrating his father's illness. It should be in honour of the Bourbon family who were now living as exiles in England. For the occasion, George created himself Field Marshal and reinstated Frederick as Commander-in-Chief, and resplendent in their new uniforms, thus greeted their guests. Oddly enough, most of the French royalty gravitated towards Edward and Julie, for there was a deep friendship between them. Lady Hertford, gleaming with satin and diamonds, watched them spitefully. She had expected to be the centre of attraction, she being the Regent's hostess. It had given her great satisfaction that Maria Fitzherbert had refused to accept the invitation to attend, but Maria had her pride, and rather than sit at any table other than that of George and the visiting royalty, she preferred to stay away.

The Duke of Clarence was obviously enjoying himself in the company of Catherine Tylney-Long, despite the fact that his eldest daughter, Sophia, was also a guest. Where was Mrs. Jordan? wondered Julie. No doubt hurling herself about some stage, invoking laughter and chuckles from her audience, all to help maintain her family.

Julie and Edward considered themselves fortunate that they had received an invitation, for Edward had again fallen foul of his brother. During a quarrel between George and Maria, Maria had retaliated that Edward and Julie thought his treatment of her was very bad; a rash statement that had serious repercussions when next the brothers met. Why couldn't Edward mind his own damned business? So violent did George become, that Edward had hurried home and, on Julie's advice, written to Maria, telling her:

'What has passed on this occasion renders it absolutely necessary for me to implore you, whenever I have the happiness of seeing you again, that we should never touch upon that most delicate subject—the state of things between the Prince and yourself.'

    •   •   •   •   •

What had been rumoured for so long had happened. The Duke of Clarence and Mrs. Jordan had parted . . . at the Duke's request.

Again it was Maria Fitzherbert who brought the news to Julie, voluble in her denunciation of William.

'I've always had a tender spot for the Duke of Clarence. Bit of a fool at times, but Dorothy Jordan made a man of him . . . and now . . . these royal brothers!'

'How . . . how long has he and Mrs. Jordan . . . ?'

'Been together? Over twenty years, and many a time I've heard her say, they've never had a serious quarrel . . .'

Julie was hardly listening. Twenty years together . . . about the same time as she and Edward . . . and now separation. Could it happen to her and Edward? No. No. No.

Maria was still chattering . . . 'and he actually went straightway to Miss Tylney-Long and proposed, saying Mrs. Jordan had been a perfect angel and would put no obstruction in their way . . . in fact Mrs. Jordan was all for the marriage.'

'And did the lady accept him?'

Maria laughed. 'She's giving the matter her consideration, or rather she's listening to her Mama's persuasion. Mama, it would appear, is the keener of the two to enter royal circles.'

'And Mrs. Jordan? What is to become of her?'

'She is to have care of the girls while the boys remain at Bushey under the care of a tutor.'

'And Mrs. Jordan herself? Is she distressed?'

'Dorothy Jordan is an actress; able to hide her feelings. She is making it known that it is only money . . . or rather the lack of it . . . that has decided the Duke. He is so heavily in debt that he would welcome the extra allowance marriage would bring him, whether his bride was an heiress or not.'

Marriage. Extra allowance. Heavy debts. Julie felt a sinking feeling in the pit of her stomach. It all applied to Edward. Would William's action influence Edward? Would he be on the look-out for a bride?

'Holy Mother of Jesus take pity on me,' she prayed. 'Put such thoughts from my mind.' It couldn't happen to her and Edward.

That night, she was able to talk camly with him, relieved to hear his sympathy for Mrs. Jordan and his condemnation of his brothers. Edward was so different from them. As a result of moderate living, he was fit and healthy, fond of outdoor exercise, walking and riding. True, he did dye his hair a dark brown, despite teasing that grey hair was more distinguished looking; and despite exercise, he was becoming rather corpulent.

9

Julie was writing her New Year letter to Catherine de Salaberry. They were regular correspondents, Catherine delight-
ing in hearing all the Royal Family and London gossip and
Julie revelling in hearing of the de Salaberry affairs. Now
she looked up and over to Edward. 'Have you any message
for Louis and dear Souris?'

'Depends on what you have already written.' He rose and
came over, standing by her chair, reading the letter.

He pulled up a stool, seated himself, and wrote: '*I am
sure you will be pleased to know that what our life was
when we were beside you, that it has continued during
the twenty years that have passed since we left Canada
and I love to think that twenty years hence it may be the
same.*'

She looked up at him, the love shining in her eyes. 'Thank
you, *mon ami*, thank you.' She drew his head down and
kissed him, and feeling the tears on her cheeks, he drew her
up, his arms around her, kissing her tenderly, holding her
tight.

She offered up a prayer of thanksgiving. She felt safe.
Poor Maria Fitzherbert. Poor Dorothy Jordan.

.   .   .   .   .

She was crossing the hall preparatory to going out to her
carriage when a muffled sound from the library caused her

to stop and listen. She never disturbed Edward in the morning, but what was the strange noise? It sounded like sobbing. It was sobbing. Edward sobbing.

She flung open the door and then, still holding the knob, stared at Edward, his head on the desk covered by his hands, with great muffled sobs escaping between his fingers.

She was down on her knees beside him. 'What is it, Edward, what is it?'

Without lifting his head, he indicated a paper on his desk. From her kneeling position she attempted to read it but it only appeared to be a list of names. He was trying to speak, but the only word that escaped him was 'Edward . . . Edward . . . Edward.'

As though struck by an icy blast, she shivered with sudden understanding. She rose and studied the list on the desk. There it was, just one name standing out from all the others, as though written in letters of blood, a list of casualties . . . and among them Lieutenant Edward de Salaberry . . . killed at Bajdos.

She flung herself down, her head on Edward's knee, bursting into an uncontrollable torrent of tears. As though realising her need for comfort, Edward's own grief began to ease as he caressed Julie's hair, but neither could find words to express their heart-break.

At last, exhausted, she allowed her woman to take her to her room; to accept a mild opiate, but she could not sleep. A small, eager boy was with her all the time, teasing her about her wig; excitedly gazing about the theatre from the privacy of their box, asking to be allowed to send the satin programme home to his mother; winding up first one mechanical device then another . . . she and Edward were at the christening party . . . they were the baby's godparents . . .

. . . . . .

153

Napoleon had abdicated, and now exiled on the Isle of Elba, he could no longer terrorise Europe. There was jubilation throughout all England, the signal for the festivities to begin. For the rich there were again series of carnivals, balls and assemblies, while the poor had their village feasts and fairs, their ox-roasting and firework displays, all to celebrate the restoration of the Bourbon family to France, Louis XVIII, the brother of the guillotined king, emerging from his exile in Buckinghamshire, to be brought to London in great pomp and state. The two obese gentlemen, the Regent and Louis, rode in the Regent's carriage drawn by eight white horses, the postillions wearing the Bourbon colours, golden fleur-de-lis on a white background. Alongside, together with other gentlemen, Edward rode his favourite charger.

There was a reception at Carlton House, Edward being one of the first to be presented to Louis. Three days later, Louis left London with Edward and his brother, the Duke of Sussex, riding by the carriage windows, until they reached Dover. There with ten thousand voices bidding him farewell and God-speed, Louis returned to his country, the Regent, the Duke of Kent and the Duke of Sussex standing on the pier, bowing ceremoniously.

•   •   •   •   •

Hardly had the Bourbon bunting been removed, than the Russian and Prussian colours were being draped across the streets to welcome the Tsar of Russia and the King of Prussia. More state processions, each of the royal brothers riding in his own carriage.

In the salons of the great, down to the gin shops and the streets, gossip and rumour were rife. Where was the Princess of Wales? Was it true she was going abroad? And the eighteen-year-old Princess Charlotte? Would she marry the Crown Prince of Orange or did she now prefer the Prince

Frederick of Prussia? And that good-looking young prince in the Tsar's entourage, Leopold of Coburg, just why had he come?

Now preparations were being made to honour the Duke of Wellington for his great victories. Although Julie had no heart for the coming celebrations, she knew she must be at Edward's side.

As yet she had not been able to write to Monsieur and Madame de Salaberry. She was waiting for their grief to subside.

It seemed incredible, incredibly cruel, that Fate could strike at the same family in so short a time, but just before the Wellington reception at Carlton House, information reached Edward that Maurice and Chevalier de Salaberry had both died in India of a fever.

Julie was almost demented with grief. For days she shut herself in her room regardless of Edward's suffering. How could she ever write to Catherine again? What could she say that would comfort her friend? It was easier for Edward, she argued. He was busy helping to organise this Wellington reception, to be the most brilliant occasion of the year. She had no wish to go; every uniformed man would be a reminder of the three dead de Salaberry boys.

It took the combined efforts of several of her friends to point out that the de Salaberrys were a military family of several generations back. They would accept the deaths in true military tradition and courage.

All the members of the Royal Family were present to honour the victor, the Regent accompanying his mother the Queen, followed by all his brothers and sisters, even the Duchess of York coming out from her country retreat at Oatlands, to stand by her husband.

Julie was glad that her presence was of little consequence. She could arouse no enthusiasm to glorify war. All she could do was to pray for the safety of Charles de Salaberry, now much in the news for his courage and prowess in fighting against the Americans. 'Please God,' she prayed, 'spare them this one son.'

It grieved Edward to see her so dejected; declining all invitations; refusing to entertain in what should have been a most splendid season. When, however, he announced that he had invited Prince Leopold to dinner, he refused to listen to her objections.

'It will be good for us, *ma petite*. He is young . . . handsome. We need young company . . .'

She had been surprised that she had enjoyed the evening, taking an immediate liking to the Prince. He was quite frank about his hopes. He had come to ask the Regent for the hand of his daughter. He had met Charlotte on several occasions, but so far, he had not received any encouragement from either the lady or her father. Could the Duke of Kent help? Julie gave Edward a warning look . . . a look which clearly meant 'Keep out', to be answered by an understanding smile, the first for many days.

He was a frequent visitor after that evening, Edward taking a fancy to the young man who, lodging in one room in High Street, Mary-le-bone, appreciated the comfort and luxury of Castle Hill Lodge.

It was a pity he had to leave England hurriedly, on the occasion of the death of his brother in-law, but before going Edward arranged to act as postman between him and Charlotte, the Regent being very hostile to Leopold's proposal.

* * * * *

It was late September before Julie could bring herself to write to Catherine de Salaberry and only then because Catherine had written telling her of Charles' marriage and the birth of a baby daughter.

'*Alas, I had a great desire to write, but I felt I could not do so without exposing my afflicted friend La Souris to a*

156

*blow that might be fatal. It was necessary to act with
prudence and I have waited until the time would arrive
when I might write without increasing her grief. I hope
that her health might be restored and that religion in giving
her the consoling hope that she will again see her children
in a better world will relieve the anguish of her heart. My
memory will always recall Quebec and Beauport and a
friendship which has triumphed over twenty years of absence. All the public papers here are full of the great deeds
of Colonel Charles de Salaberry ... I wish you to give him
a thousand remembrances from me and to thank him for
having given my name to his first-born.'*

.   .   .   .   .

The Battle of Waterloo had been fought and won but the
victorious army, back home and disbanded, found another
adversary to contend with: the war against poverty and
unemployment. Edward, as patron of many charities,
found his time fully occupied.

He had of recent years become acquainted with a certain
Robert Owen, a wealthy Scots cotton manufacturer, whose
ideas caused other manufacturers to scoff with derision. He
provided his workers with well built houses and arranged
that so many of their working hours were spent in agricul-
tural work, growing their own food. Educational facilities
were available for all, the result being that there were few
misdemeanours in their model settlement. When his com-
petitors derided him, he deplored their greed and lack of
concern for the employment of children and sweated
labour.

Edward was all enthusiasm, inviting Mr. Owen to Kensington Palace, and attending his lectures in Bedford Square,
agreeing with him on the evil of a depressed working
class.

When certain peers tackled him on his radical views,

Edward was quick to retort that his politics were no secret, nor was he ashamed of them, stressing, *'I foresee results. I know that there will be a much more just equality of our race and an equality that will give much more security and happiness to all than does the present system.'*

He was now giving donations even more liberally than before, despite his inability to pay his debts. Although he was receiving a total income of £24,000 he still found it impossible not to incur further debts, blaming the heavy interest he had to pay his creditors; the fact that taxation took £2,000 and that recently his solicitor had absconded with £2,000 he had handed to him for insurance.

Now his creditors of long standing were beginning to ask for repayment of capital; payment of interest was not enough. Frantically, he borrowed from close friends including Robert Owen, but as quickly as he paid one rapacious shop-keeper, another demanded his dues. Desperately he wrote his brother the Regent. Surely he would help.

My Dear Brother,

The recollection of those habits of unreserved confidence, which it was my good fortune to have with you in former days . . as ever being my steadiest friend in many of the most trying moments of my life, renders it impossible for me to leave it to your ministers to be the first to acquaint you . . . of an official appeal to your justice for relief at a moment when overwhelmed with embarrassments. I could no longer refrain from taking that step. I am sure that you will judge my claim from your own upright, just mind and good heart, as then I cannot doubt of the result being favourable in my interest. With every sentiment of warmest devotion and attachment, I remain, my dearest brother,

Your faithful and affectionate, Edward.

Julie had shaken her head in doubt when he handed her

the letters before despatch. He relied so much on her judgement and insight, that he consulted her in all personal matters.

'I do not like the tone, *mon ami*. There is a falseness . . . you are debasing yourself . . .'

For once he was angry, blustering, 'Nonsense. George and I are friends. He knows what it is to have a millstone of debt around his neck. It was only to clear his debts that he married Princess Caroline . . .' He stopped suddenly, noticing the odd, wary look in her expression.

So that was one way a royal duke could clear his debts. Marriage to a princess. Dear God, was that in Edward's mind? Would George suggest that way out?

The bluster in his voice had increased. 'Let him refuse, if he so wishes; I shall then transfer my request to the government; they cannot refuse me!'

'No? What gives you so much confidence, Sir?'

'To begin with, how many equipments did I lose while on active service? Seven, Madame, seven at a cost of more than £30,000 . . . some of them not yet paid for . . .'

'Edward, *mon ami*, would it not be better if we were to live in more simple style? We do not need four establishments. I am prepared to forgo your allowance of £1,000 . . .'

'Enough, Madame, enough. Why should we live like paupers? Like a village squire? I am a prince and I intend to live as a prince. As to your allowance. I have always regretted that it was so low. My brother still gives Mrs. Fitzherbert £6,000 even now they are parted . . .'

'But he is the Regent, Sir . . .'

Edward, however, was adamant and the letter was sent. When the reply came, it was from the Prime Minister, the Earl of Liverpool, George disdaining to answer it. The earl refused all help.

Not to be outdone, Edward then tackled the Home Secretary, Lord Sidmouth, who had been Prime Minister at the time of the Gibraltar affair. Surely he could recall the excellent work he had done on the Rock? Lord Sidmouth could only remember the Duke's extreme severity and regretted that he could offer no assistance.

As a final effort he put before the government the cost of his lost equipments, claiming compensation. Back came the terse reply that the army regulations did not allow for such losses.

It was Robert Owen who eventually came to his aid, endorsing Julie's suggestion that they should live more within their means, unless His Highness wished to find himself in the Bankruptcy Court.

From his annual income Mr. Owen proposed that Edward should hand over £17,000 each year to two trustees, William Allen and Joseph Hume, both rich, trustworthy business associates, who would gradually pay off the Duke's debts within six years.

Julie was all enthusiasm for the idea. In a few years' time, Edward would be free of debt.

'But that leaves me with but £7,000. . . .'

'Ample, sir. Ample. Which house shall we maintain, sir?'

Edward groaned. 'I cannot part with Castle Hill Lodge . . .'

'Then Castle Hill it shall be, but do we need such a vast household . . . such an enormous staff . . . ?'

'You will next be suggesting that I should carry the coal, and you will do the cooking. . . .'

'It would be a diverting experience, Sir . . . but seriously, Sir, I see no need for more than one coach. . . .'

'Be quiet, woman, I know I am fond of walking but as a prince and a gentleman . . .'

'Do you need all those horses, Sir? I know you are fond of riding, but you can ride but one horse at a time . . .'

The wrangling went on for several days, at times with all due seriousness, but most often Julie's gay humour leavening the dour prospect. They would continue to live at Castle

Hill Lodge, Edward keeping but one horse, and Julie's allowance being reduced to £400, and no longer would they maintain a box at Drury Lane.

.   .   .   .   .

It was no use. Try as he would; depriving himself of almost everything that made life worth living, Edward could not live on £7,000 a year. There was nothing for it but to leave England and live on the Continent, where the cost of living was much cheaper. Leaving Julie to pack, Edward went to Brussels where he succeeded in finding a house at the low rent of £300 a year. It was, however, in a bad state of repair and decoration, involving several months' labour, and forgetful that his aim in coming to Brussels was to save money, he borrowed a considerable sum to make the place fit for Julie and himself to live in.

.   .   .   .   .

The love affairs of Princess Charlotte had resolved themselves. She was now Her Royal Highness Princess Charlotte of Saxe-Coburg.

Inside the great Crimson Room of Carlton House, where the marriage had just been solemnised, Edward gazed around at his family; his diminutive mother, unable to resist the frequent pinch of snuff, standing beside the Regent, gross but resplendent in his Field Marshal's uniform; his brothers, the Dukes of York and Clarence already well laced with brandy, and scarcely steady on their feet; his sisters agleam with diamonds, yet looking so pathetic; no air of gaiety about them. Why in the name of God didn't they get married?

As for the bride, he felt a lump in his throat each time he looked her way, so beautiful in her gown and jewels; happiness radiating from her sparkling eyes. He was glad she was now married; away from the tyranny, the lechery and the dissipation of Carlton House. Leopold would make her happy. Poor child to be deprived of her mother on her wedding day, for Caroline was now gallivanting all over the Continent, making a fool of herself.

He was aware that Charlotte was attempting to attract his attention. On going over to her she took his arm and moved him out of earshot. She was bubbling over with happiness. 'Uncle Edward, I do so want to thank you for everything you did. Without you, I'd still be unmarried, pining my heart out . . .'

'Say no more, Charlotte. I am happy for both of you . . .'

'Our only wish, dear Uncle, is that Leopold and I could help you in some way . . .' She paused, tapping her foot, and then continued hesitantly, 'Leopold and I think it would be an excellent match if you were to marry his sister, Victoire. She is a widow . . . only thirty years of age. Leopold could arrange everything. . . .'

'Princess! Please! I have no wish to marry . . .'

'I know Madame de St. Laurent is most charming, but if you married . . .'

'Princess! I must ask you to say no more. I find it most distasteful . . .'

She shrugged her shoulders. 'Very well. I only wished to help. You are not vexed, are you, Uncle?'

'How could one be vexed with you on your wedding-day? Say no more, dear child. Forget it.'

But Edward could not forget it, and it wasn't until he was in his carriage, weary and longing for Castle Hill, that the full impact struck him. What was it Charlotte had said? 'Leopold and I . . . ?' So the matter had been under discussion. The impudence of the pair of them, especially Leopold. He had been Julie's guest; she had made him welcome; had taken a liking to him; had encouraged their love affair, and all the time he was planning to upset his and Julie's connection; planning that he should marry his widowed sister! Blast his impudence. No man—nor woman—was going to order his life.

· · · · · ·

After the excitement of the royal wedding, the tenor of London life appeared to fall flat, especially for Edward and Julie, now biding their time before going to Brussels. In an effort to revive a spirit of gaiety, Mrs. Fitzherbert gave a ball and supper at her London house in Tylney Street, inviting all the royal dukes. Yet Julie continued to feel low-spirited.

'Come now. my dear Julie, Brussels is not so far away . . . I shall be a constant visitor . . .'

'And no one will be more welcome than you, dear Maria . . . but 'tis not the parting . . . I feel that I shall never live in England again . . .'

'Nonsense. As soon as Edward has his affairs in order, back you will come. Edward has already assured me of that. He is not taking the house on a long lease, is he?'

'No . . . but then why is he spending so much . . . ? And again the house will not be ready until October. I feel most uneasy.'

With a succession of partners, Julie quickly recovered her good spirits, but Edward remained morose and quiet. '' Twill be a good thing, Madame, when he gets to Brussels. He needs a change,' was the Duke of Clarence's laconic comment.

She felt an impish desire to ask him if he had yet found a wife, for his pursuit of ladies and his rejected proposals were a standing joke. She still considered his parting from Mrs. Jordan most unjustifiable, but then, she told herself, she was biased, being in the same insecure position herself. Instead, she asked after his children, and was instantly deluged in a stream of anecdotes about the most beautiful gifted children God had ever created.

163

'How he loves them,' she thought wistfully . . . 'if only . . .'

'And you will be shortly leaving us, Madame . . . ?'

'Regretfully, yes. But first I am going to Paris to stay with my sister, the Comtesse de Jenac. I have not seen her since the Revolution . . . Edward is going to travel for about a month . . . looking up old acquaintances . . .'

'Ah . . . ah . . . ah . . .' Finding William's insinuating, leering laugh distasteful, she pleaded fatigue and asked to be taken back to Mrs. Fitzherbert.

Mrs. Jordan was living in Paris, she mused. She must pay her a call.

A month later, there was a gigantic dinner for two thousand held at the Mansion House. It was the occasion of bestowing the Freedom of London on the Duke of Kent, the Duke of Sussex and Prince Leopold; the scrolls being presented in gold boxes. If there were two thousand inside the Banqueting Hall, there were twice as many again outside, not so much to gaze at the ageing, obese dukes as to see the new-fangled gas lights, lighting up the roadway and entrance, and for those who could get near enough to see, the Hall itself.

Edward's hope that his sisters would marry had come about for one of them, thirty-eight-year-old Mary, who had married her cousin, William Frederick, Duke of Gloucester. Edward was disgusted. 'Why has the Regent allowed it?' he complained to Julie. 'The man's an imbecile . . . he's known as "Silly Billy". She'd have been better off remaining single.'

It was Mrs. Fitzherbert, coming to dine at Castle Hill for the last time, who brought the news: Dorothy Jordan was dead. She had died alone in Paris, save for one faithful servant.

'But why?' protested Julie. 'All those children. Could not one of them have been there?'

'They are all too busy with their own affairs . . .'

'But the Duke?'

'She was too proud to let him know the state of her affairs.

Poor William. He wept bitterly when he brought the news to me.'

'Poor William,' thought Julie angrily. 'Poor Mrs. Jordan.'

．　　　．　　　．　　　．　　　．

They left Castle Hill Lodge towards the end of August. Their plans were made; Julie to stay in Paris with her sister until Edward joined her, going together to Brussels as soon as the house was ready.

For some time prior to their decision to leave England, Julie's twelve-year-old nephew had been living under their care, attending a school in Ealing but going to the Lodge at the weekends. It was a great source of joy for both of them to have the boy about the house, consequently their impending departure had caused a certain amount of consternation.

It was Frederick Wetherall, now General Wetherall, who had come to the rescue. Over the years, he and his family had become very close friends of Edward and Julie, having a house not too far away and being in Edward's confidence in almost all his private affairs.

'May I remind you, Sir . . . and Madame . . . that my son Alexander is at school in Brussels . . .'

'Why, of course . . .'

'Then what more satisfactory arrangement, that I make myself responsible for the well-being of Master Mongenet . . . and you for my son.'

'Splendid. Splendid. We shall indeed enjoy having the boy, shall we not, Madame?'

Julie was only too happy to agree. To come alive, a house needed children.

．　　　．　　　．　　　．　　　．

It was wonderful to be with her sister again; to reminisce

about their childhood; to recall and relate outstanding events in their individual lives; to go shopping; to visit the theatre, yet she was lonely without Edward. There was a family reunion, her brother Jean-Claude and his two sons, Claude-Charles and Charles-Benjamin, joining them, but it was not until Edward arrived, and she was able to present her family to him, that she felt the party was complete.

Immediately they were inundated with invitations from the French Royal Family to visit and dine with them, Louis remembering England's hospitality and their recent heart-warming send-off. It was all very regal and splendid but Julie was longing to see her new home; to settle down and live their own quiet lives again.

It was towards the end of October before they arrived in Brussels. Julie was entranced. Under Edward's instructions, the house had been transformed into a most desirable residence, the outside gleaming fresh with whitewash and paint, the inside richly carpeted and decorated. There was a flower-garden, lawns, an orchard and, to Julie's amazement, extensive stabling.

'But, Edward, I thought . . .'

'You thought I was going to continue with but one horse? *Non, non, ma chérie*. I have brought my stallion . . . he will make much money for me. I have to have other horses for my curricle . . . my barouche. I have to have stablemen . . . coachmen . . . Have no fears, *ma petite* . . . all will be well.'

Soon there were invitations from the Brussels Court and they, too, began to entertain on a modest scale, theatre parties, whist parties, dinner parties. Edward had not abandoned his work for the English charitable concerns, for each week the English Embassy brought him at least one hundred and fifty letters, and to assist him, Edward had to engage a private secretary, and still needed the help of two army sergeants!

Within a very short time they had established a gentle,

relaxed routine, Julie happy with her needlework, studying her *Journals de la mode*; Edward seemingly content with his work, his books and his horses.

Christmas came and went, Julie and the Duke enjoying the revels of all the houses that flung open their doors for them. Then it was Spring, and the garden came to life, became a riot of colour to welcome Maria Fitzherbert when, true to her promise, she came to visit them. By the time they had been there a year, Julie was recognised as a delightful, considerate hostess and Edward a reliable helper in any charitable concern. Soon it would be Christmas again, their second away from England, yet neither yearning to go back.

/

•   •   •   •   •

Brussels had been enveloped in fog all the previous night, and with it still persisting on the sabbath morn, few families had ventured out to church. It was most maddening that when they heard a horse galloping along their cobbled street, they could see nothing from their windows, except 'someone on horseback' going going towards the Duke's place.

Edward and Julie looked up in surprise as the caller was announced; a courier from England . . . a special courier. The look that passed getween them was of bewilderment . . . then of fear as Edward ripped open the letter, taking one brief look, and then pushing it into Julie's hand, with a choking monosyllable, 'Charlotte', before going to the window to stare out into the fog. They knew she and Leopold were awaiting the birth of their first child . . . and now . . . the child, a boy, had been stillborn, and Charlotte, dear little Charlotte, was dead.

Julie went over and joined Edward, putting her arm through his, but unable to speak a word. Suddenly Edward turned, almost shouting, 'I know what caused it. All that damned bleeding . . . the all-round, invincible cure. Mrs.

Fitzherbert told us they were bleeding her, all those months ago. Poor little Princess . . .'

'Poor Prince Leopold,' whispered Julie.

.   .   .   .   .

She was lying on her bed; a bright fire in the grate, but with the drapes drawn. What had happened? Quickly her memory came flooding back. She had been to mass. It was terribly cold. Back home, Edward had already breakfasted. While the footman had poured her tea, she had glanced at a newspaper. . . . Oh God . . . oh God . . . so it was true. The newspaper had an article saying the unmarried dukes should all marry immediately—and so beget heirs for the throne. Not Edward. No, not Edward. William was the elder. William was already a father ten times. William was a certainty . . .

She remembered crying out . . . falling to the floor . . . and then Edward carrying her upstairs . . . and leaving her to the ministrations of her woman. Why didn't he come to her now; put her mind to rest; assure her that she had no cause to pester herself? Did the idea of taking a wife, a younger woman, of having a child, intrigue him? Why didn't he come? She wouldn't let him go. Why should she? They had been together for twenty-seven years. Oh, she knew she was wicked, possessive and jealous, but the thought of Edward with another woman in his arms, making love to her, getting her with child . . . a child he would be proud to show to the world. No. No. No. But even as she cried the words aloud, she knew they were futile. She had no hold on Edward . . . not even their love. She found herself weeping noisily, burying her head in the pillow to stifle the sobs, but when all the tears were spent, a gentle calmness took over. What had been her last thoughts? Not even their love could hold him? If only he would come to her now, take her in his arms, and whisper, 'Don't cry, *ma petite*. I

168

will never leave you. I love you too much.' Then she could be brave; kiss him tenderly and gently push him away, saying, 'And I love you, *mon brave* . . . but you must marry for the sake of your country.' That was all she asked. That he should go on loving her even though they were apart. Whatever happened, whoever he married, no other woman could ever know the joy of sharing Edward's youth; he was almost fifty now. They had loved and made love for the sheer joy of it; not at the urging of a government or newspaper with the hope of begetting a child.

She must have fallen asleep, for it was some time later when she found Edward bending over her saying, 'Feeling better, *ma petite*? Take no notice of that stupid newspaper . . . you know how the papers exaggerate!'

'But, Edward, if it is your duty . . .' The tears began again, and Edward gently took her hand. 'Listen, Julie. Naturally, I've been giving the matter some thought. Now William is the elder and as you know he is desirous of marrying . . .'

'But so far, no one desires to be the Duchess of Clarence . . .'

'Ah, but the circumstances have now changed, and I have decided to wait until about March, to give William the first opportunity . . .'

Somehow the statement jarred. Opportunity? What was it to be, a game of chance between the royal brothers? And there had been no reassurance.

$\cdot \qquad \cdot \qquad \cdot \qquad \cdot \qquad \cdot \qquad \cdot$

The Duke had immediately put his household into mourning. At first he was undecided as to whether he should go over to England for the funeral, but as neither command nor request came from the Regent, he had decided to remain in Brussels. Actually, he was feeling somewhat ashamed of himself. When he had read the article that had brought about Julie's swoon, he had felt a wave of excitement. So the country was looking towards him! It was then that he recalled the gypsy in Gibraltar. 'You will have a daughter ... she will be a queen.' Yes, he must marry, but what would become of his dear Julie? Of course, with his increased allowance, he would be able to provide for her on a generous scale ... but he still loved her ... He would write to Mrs. Fitzherbert. She was a woman of experience.

'Unfortunately the same mail that brought me the overwhelming tidings of the dreadful catastrophe at Claremont also brought a copy of the morning chronicle in which the editor in the broadest and I conceive most indelicate manner calls the attention of the country on me ... Thank God, owing to my abstemious mode of living ... I have preserved my health but my heart is half-broke and when I look on my poor companion ... and I think ere long be forced by my duties to part, it quite distresses me and from morning till night I hardly ever have a dry eye ... I feel I ought to wait what may be my Naval brother's plan ... and being my elder must be first thought on. Yet even that can only be thought on if the means are afforded me—amply to provide for that individual who has been my sole comfort and companion during so many dreary years.'

Christmas was torture for them, both knowing it was the last they would spend together. They accepted no invitations; they entertained no one. All Europe was watching and waiting. Would the Duke of Kent marry? Already the name of the lady, Princess Victoire Maria Louise was being spoken of as the most likely bride.

While consultations were going on between London and Coburg, Edward wrote several letters to Auguste Vasserot, Baron de Vincy, the friend of Geneva days.

Dear Vincy,
    ... I have in fact been living for more than two months in complete seclusion ... I have hardly seen a living soul

. . . My faithful companion, to whom I have read the paragraph of your letter which concerns her, is very alive to all the complimentary remarks which you make in regard to her. She is, thank God, in good health, although she has profoundly shared all my grief during these last two months of seclusion . . . She has become dearer to me, if such a thing were possible, by her conduct during this wretched time.

Edward. Duke of Kent.

.   .   .   .   .

Edward and General Wetherall were now exchanging letters with greater frequency and as it had always been the practice for Julie to read them, Edward had to beg of the General never to mention the proposed marriage, knowing how it disturbed her. Not to show her the letters would rouse her suspicions.

His mind was in a state of great confusion. Deep down, the prospect of marriage with a thirty-year-old bride excited him. To hold his own children in his arms . . . the very thought of it sent his blood pulsating, but it was an excitement over-ridden with guilt. How could he dismiss Julie? Whenever the matter was mentioned between them, he still maintained that he would only marry in the event of his brother William failing to do so . . . and then only because duty to his country demanded it. He despised himself for being such a liar for already he had set the wheels in motion; already instructed the government to ask for the hand of Princess Victoire. He was a coward . . . he dare not tell Julie . . . but dear God . . . that was because of his love for her . . . his desire not to hurt her.

Now the pace began to quicken. The Princess had accepted, dependent upon various legal formalities. Hastily, he wrote General Wetherall, that under the subterfuge that he required his signature on certain documents pertaining to his property he should write and ask him to return to London as soon as possible.

The ruse worked, Julie reading the letter without suspecting any ulterior motive.

'How long will you be gone, Sir?'

He felt a sudden impulse to take her in his arms, to shout out for the world to hear, 'I'm not going. I intend to stay with you for the rest of my life,' but the die was cast. Honour demanded that he should now marry the Princess.

He shrugged his shoulders. 'Possibly several weeks, *ma petite*, for I shall be expected to remain for my sister Elizabeth's birthday. Why do you not visit your sister in Paris?'

She regarded him steadily. 'A very good idea, Sir.'

•   •   •   •   •

The two carriages were drawn up at the front of the house, footmen carrying cases and valises, some to one carriage, some to the other, when Julie, ready for departure, became aware of Philip Beck hovering around as though desirous of speaking with her.

'Yes, Philip, what is it?'

The man swallowed. 'If I may be permitted, Madame . . . 'tis just to bid you goodbye . . .'

So what she had guessed was true. This was goodbye. She held out her hand. 'Why, yes . . . till we meet again . . .' Did that whispering voice belong to her? She could feel her lips trembling as she went on, in an almost inaudible voice, 'You . . . you will take good care of the Duke, will you not?'

She could see the tears in his eyes, unable to speak. Mustering her courage, she essayed, 'I . . . I want to thank you for your devoted service to . . . to us both . . . twenty-eight years is it not? Who would have guessed all those years ago, when you came to Malaga to escort me back to Gibraltar, that . . . that . . .' Her voice broke.

'Madame, dear Madame, I never thought . . .'

'Ah, there you are, Beck. Are all my valises stowed away?'
Edward's voice boomed across the hall.

Philip Beck made to lift her hand, then, remembering,
asked, 'May I have the honour, Madame?' Overcome, she
nodded in acquiescence, smiling tearfully as he kissed her
hand. Thank God, Edward had interrupted them before she
broke down. Edward took her hand as he escorted her to
the carriage. There must be no scene in front of the servants. Taking her in his arms, he kissed her gently. '*Au
revoir, ma petite.*'

For a moment she clung to him. 'Take great care of yourself, *mon amour*. You are not yet entirely rid of your heavy
cold,' and then she was in the carriage, the footmen putting
up the steps. She remained at the window, her eyes never
leaving him until they rounded the bend, then sank back
allowing the flood of tears to break through the barrier of
her grief.

•   •   •   •   •

Edward, in his carriage, taking the road for Calais, gave a
sigh of relief. How he admired her . . . still loved her. How
he pitied her, for her grief over the last few weeks had been
such that she had scarcely ate or slept, dreading the possi-
bility of parting.

How would she react when she learned they would never
meet again? That soon he would be married to the Princess
Victoire? That he had parted from her by means of a ruse
. . . but dear God in Heaven, he could never have found
the courage to tell her.

He would see to it she had an ample allowance . . .
enough for servants and a carriage. He would write to their
mutual friends, the Duc d'Orléans, de Vincy, General
Wetherall, asking them to call on Madame whenever in
Paris . . . to continue their friendship. It would take time, of
course, for her to regain her normal happy, gay personality

but with good friends around . . . and her family . . . He would write this very night, telling her the truth, regretting the subterfuge, begging her forgiveness . . . assuring her that he would love her to eternity . . .

.   .   .   .   .

Edward, her beloved Duke, was now the husband of the German princess. The Parisian newspapers were full of the antics of English royalty . . . three elderly dukes having taken young brides all bent on producing an heir. There were crude, vulgar lampoons but they made no impression whatsoever on her; she was too stunned. She had known of the imminence of the marriage; believed she was prepared for it, capable of holding her emotions in check, yet when she heard it had taken place, she was in a state of collapse; broken, crushed and confused.

Despite having a radiant bride at his side, Edward could not rid himself of the feeling of guilt, again writing to de Vincy.

My Dear de Vincy,
I shall not conceal from you my separation from my excellent and faithful companion of almost twenty-eight years cost me a far greater sacrifice than it would ever be possible for me to express to you . . . the friendship produced by so long an intimacy will never diminish. Nothing can alter the sentiments we mutually entertain for each other. When any of my friends is within easy reach of this excellent woman, I desire that they give any mark of attention they can show to her and that they take their wives to call on her to whom I owe so much during so many consecutive years and above all in this last crisis. Were I to live to the age of Methuselah, I should never be able to discharge my debt. She has resumed her family name and is now styled Comtesse de Mongenet and that she now re-

sides in the Hôtel de Ste. Aldegonde, 116 rue de Grenelle, Paris.

.　　.　　.　　.　　.

For a long time, she refused to see all callers but when the Marquis de Permangle was announced, a flicker of interest came into her eyes. So he was alive! He had escaped from Madame Guillotine!

Quickly she ordered her woman to fetch a fresh gown and a newly dressed wig. She regarded herself critically in the tall pier-glass, not that she had any desire to re-enslave her old lover, but wondering whether he would recognise her, now nearing sixty . . . plump and of sorrowful expression.

She found herself curtseying to a round-shouldered, portly gentleman whose face also told of much suffering.

'Sir, I am indeed grateful for your calling . . .'

' 'Twas the Duc d'Orléans who acquainted me . . .'

'And all these years, I have been wondering. I heard that you had been arrested . . .'

'I was in Les Carmes prison for eighteen months, waiting to be executed . . .'

'Then how did you escape?'

He shrugged his shoulders. 'I was fortunate. A good friend . . . though a revolutionary . . . saw my name on the list due for execution and smuggled me out of a side-door.'

'The Holy Mother be thanked. But why did you leave the safety of Malaga?'

'Why does a man return to his native country . . . to his estates? But you, dear lady? I have heard much of your great sorrows.'

'. . . and my years of happiness, too, I hope,' she said quietly.

'Quite so, Madame, which makes your present state so woeful . . .'

'Tell me about yourself,' she interrupted quickly.

'Well, to begin with, I am now married and have a son . . .'

'Then I am indeed happy for you . . . and your wife . . .'

'With your permission, Ma'am, I would bring her to call on you.'

'I should be enchanted . . .'

It was this visit of Claude-Phillipe that marked the end of her seclusion. She began to welcome callers; to accept invitations and, in return, to entertain.

It was most unfortunate that shortly afterwards, her sister died. For a while, Julie vacillated as to what she should do. Uppermost in her mind was the thought of returning to Canada to renew her friendship with the de Salaberrys. She was still in a state of indecision when she heard of the birth of Edward's daughter bringing back the heart-ache and misery. Humbly she made confession. She knew she was wicked to harbour such feelings, for deep within her, she desired that Edward should be happy. He had been an unfortunate man; he had suffered much. Perhaps now, the clouds were lifting for him.

·　　·　　·　　·　　·

It was Charles-Benjamin, now living in Paris, who brought the news to her. Edward, Duke of Kent was dead. For a moment, the room whirled around her. She attempted to rise from her chair; strong arms lifted her and placed her on the day-bed. Regaining her senses, she gazed at Charles-Benjamin in bewilderment, and then remembering, burst into a paroxysm of sobs. Never to see him again. Though she would not admit it before, one of the reasons that held her from returning to Canada was she disliked the idea of putting the Atlantic between them. Sometimes, she had argued, she would surely be able to see him at various functions. Now he was gone for ever. Damn that German frau! She had not known how to look after him. He had suffered a chill, the papers reported. And what had that woman done about it? Oh yes, Edward would say, 'Don't fuss. Nothing but a cold.' She would have known what to do with him. She understood those colds and chills. Ah, dear God, she knew what had killed him. That useless wife of his had allowed the doctors to bleed him. That was it. Edward didn't believe in bleeding. Said it weakened the patient. 'Ah, *mon chéri* . . . *mon âme* . . . how I loved you . . . the world is empty for me now.'

. . . . .

It was several weeks before she received the letter from Maria Fitzherbert. Maria, too, was deeply distressed because, save for the occasion Edward had visited her when in England for his second marriage ceremony, she had neither seen nor heard from him.

She suspected it was because of the Duchess, a very arrogant Prussian princess who could not demean herself by meeting a discarded mistress. Again it was said, she was very domineering. Poor Edward. He was not accustomed to being overruled. Worst of all, despite an increase of £6,000 in his yearly allowance, it appeared his financial difficulties had become more pressing than ever. He and his bride had lived on the Continent until the baby was almost due, only coming back to England so that the child could be born here.

He had tried to sell Castle Hill and failing an offer of any size, had hit upon the plan of selling it by lottery. Tickets were offered to the public on the understanding that all money in excess of £100,000 should go to charity. The House of Commons was most indignant that a member of the Royal Family should resort to such a scheme, and poor Edward had to drop the idea.

There was nothing for it but to get away from London where he was too accessible for his now ever-demanding creditors.

On the pretext he wanted sea-air for his baby daughter, he had rented a small furnished house at Sidmouth. There, in near poverty—the domestic staff boasted only a cook and two housemaids—he had died, and little wonder, concluded Maria, the surgeons having bled him of a hundred and twenty ounces!

⁎　　⁎　　⁎　　⁎　　⁎

Slowly peace of mind returned to her. Auguste Vasserot was not forgetful of the Duke's request and other mutual acquaintances visiting Paris always called on the Comtesse de Mongenet. General Wetherall and Philip Beck visited her to tell of Edward's last hours, both being with him to the end, both consoling her with their knowledge of the great happiness she had given him.

The French King and the royal dukes began to insist she take her place in society, so in order she could entertain on a more lavish scale, she took a house in the Rue Chanter-aine, and as in the days now gone for ever she was once again known as a hostess of distinction.

Epilogue

The doctors insisted she must stay in bed. Then, countered Julie, Comtesse de Mongenet, the bed must be taken down to her small private salon. She knew she had not long to live—and the knowledge caused her no alarm—after all, she had nearly reached her three-score years and ten. What little time was left to her, she was determined to spend where she could continually gaze at the life-size portrait of the Duke of Kent... her beloved Edward.

It was the only thing she had asked of him. True, it was really her property. She had commissioned and paid for it but there was always the danger the Duchess might object. When under General Wetherall's direction it had arrived in Paris, she had been overjoyed.

Today, there seemed to be a misty aura around the Duke's face. The usual clear-cut features appeared blurred, almost obliterating the love shining from his eyes, for the artist, aware of the great love between them, had portrayed a man happy in his domestic life.

The sound of a shot roused her from her reverie. She must have been dozing for with the rude awakening she could not recollect her surroundings. Where was she? Gibraltar or Quebec? What was all the shooting about? Another mutiny? Another execution? Dear God ... Edward ... be merciful. Then she remembered. She was in Paris. In her own salon. Then why the shooting?

She put out her thin arm, fumbling for the little silver

bell on the bedside table and when Charles Mongenet came hastening in, she asked more with curiosity than fear, 'The shooting?'

'No need to be alarmed, dear Aunt. Some madcaps playing the fool . . .'

He was a dear boy, this nephew of hers, living here with an old woman, giving her the pleasure of youthful company, since Charles-Benjamin had married and moved to Grenoble. Little did he know of the gap he had filled in her life as far away back as those Ealing schooldays.

'You wouldn't be deceiving me, would you? I'm not afraid. I'm a soldier's . . . I'm accustomed to gun-fire . . .'

'There is no danger, dear Aunt. True, there is some feeling against the King . . .'

'The Duc d'Orléans?' Now there was fear in her voice.

'No danger whatever. Wisely, he is remaining in the background.'

Dear Louis-Phillipe. No danger must come to him. He had been such a good friend to them both. How they had enjoyed his company over the years. How Edward had longed to have him as a brother-in-law but the Queen had been against his marrying the Princess Elizabeth and after several years of vain hoping, he had eventually married Princess Marie-Amélie of Sicily.

It had made no difference to their friendship. He had been the first to visit her when she arrived in Paris, heartbroken and desolate, understanding her anguish. Again, on hearing of Edward's death he had acted quickly on her behalf, writing to Thomas Coutts to act for the Comtesse de Mongenet that she should continue to receive the allowance as settled by the late Duke. Yet how could she expect it when poor Edward's debts were estimated to be in the region of £60,000?

General Wetherall and his family had been constant visitors, keeping her up-to-date with news of Castle Hill Lodge. After Edward's proposed lottery had fallen through, the contents of the house had been sold by auction. The very thought of the inquisitive, curious, gaping rabble tramping through those elegant rooms was like a knife in her heart. All the furnishings and fittings that she and Edward had chosen together; the thousands of books in his library . . . in her library; his clocks—hundreds of them; his mechanical dancing bears; his prancing horses; his fighting cocks and the myriad other mechanical gew-gaws, all sold for a few shillings to any Tom, Dick or Harry who down the years would brag, 'This belonged to the Duke of Kent, who died up to his ears in debt', and old soldiers would say, 'He was a vicious swine . . . how we hated him.'

Was Edward as vicious as they said? He was a perfectionist where military training was concerned. Early rising; long hours on the barrack square meant nothing to him, so why should his men not endure them? As for the flogging, it was odd, was it not, that after the Gibraltar affair, kicking his heels in boredom, he had been one of the first to suggest and agitate for its abolition? A strange man was her Edward, but how she had loved him!

On his most recent visit, the General had some really heart-warming news. He was now the owner of Castle Hill —or rather what was left of it for most of the handsomely carved doors and fireplaces had been sold piecemeal. A buyer had actually come forward but before he could meet the cost, he had gone bankrupt leaving the empty, denuded mansion once again desolate and ownerless. Then it was the General had stepped in, paying the demanded price to give the executors of his beloved friend a little more cash to meet the now demanding creditors. If Edward's shade was watching, how he would appreciate such true friendship.

Edward had always appreciated his friends, his affection stemming from his loveless childhood. The de Salaberrys . . . how he had loved them and their children . . . those dear boys . . . snatched away . . . perhaps Edward had been wise in denying her a family . . . but not to think of that now . . . she was grateful for the company of her nephews.

The door opened and this time Charles was accompanied by another young man who gently embraced her, asking, 'And how is my Aunt Julie today? Charles wrote you had taken to your bed, so I thought a surprise visit might be a tonic.'

'It is, dear boy, indeed it is, but,' she appeared to be thinking, '. . . isn't your wife . . . isn't she expecting to be brought to bed any time now?'

Charles-Benjamin laughed. 'There you are, Aunt Julie. Your mind is in as excellent trim as usual. Yes, my dear wife is near her time, but . . .'

She knew. They were expecting her to die and Charles had sent for Charles-Benjamin. She looked from one to the other. He was right. Her mind was quite clear and never had she felt more at peace.

.　　.　　.　　.　　.

Throughout the day and well into the night there were sporadic outbursts of shooting and the sound of marching men, but her nephews assured her there was no cause for alarm . . . indeed to the contrary . . . her dear Duc d'Orléans had been asked to be king!

The news roused her from the stupor into which she had fallen. Louis-Phillipe to be King of France! Slowly her mind winged its way over the Atlantic, back to Canada, entertaining three young Frenchmen to dinner and Edward loaning them two hundred pounds to set themselves up as schoolmasters. His goodness and concern for her had more than repaid the debt, bringing her back into the social scene when she would have shut herself away for the rest of her life.

There was no denying it, she had been a bad loser, in that

she could never put Edward from out of her mind or heart. Theirs had been a wonderful love. Why then had he forsaken her to marry the German princess?

She stirred herself to look fixedly at the portrait. Why was it so blurred these days? Where was her lorgnette . . . not that they were much help . . . ah yes . . . his features were clearer now. He was smiling . . . she could read the message behind those eyes. 'You know, Julie. You alone know and understand why I married. You knew me as no-one else ever did . . .'

As she continued to gaze, so understanding came. Throughout the whole of his life, his every action had been misconstrued, denigrated, thwarted both by his family and country. It was only his stubborn, unrelenting pride that upheld him, determined there should be one worthy achievement by which history should remember him. If he could father the heir for the English throne, would that not lift him from the morass of failures and misunderstandings? He was a healthy man of fifty while his brothers were drink-sodden lecherous degenerates. 'You do understand, *ma chérie*, do you not? You were the love of my life . . . always . . .'

Yes, she understood. She understood that pride . . . the pride that had caused her many a heart-ache . . . the pride behind which he concealed the hurt and humiliation heaped upon him. 'Oh, *mon âme . . . mon amour*,' she whispered. 'Why was Fate so cruel as to strike you down, snatching you away from the fruit of your sacrifice . . . never to enjoy the glory?' All England acclaimed the twelve-year-old Princess Victoria, but her father, the Duke of Kent, her beloved prince, was almost forgotten.

* * * * *

That His Majesty, Louis-Philippe, should call on the Comtesse de Mongenet so soon after being declared King of

France, was indeed both a surprise and honour of some magnitude.

Bowing low, Charles Mongenet essayed, 'This is indeed a great honour, Your Majesty.'

'I heard that my dear friend was ill. How is she?'

'I regret, Sir, that for much of the time, she is in a coma.'

'Would it be possible for me to see her? Is there a chance she might know me?'

'It is doubtful, Sir, but she does occasionally rally.'

'Then take me to her.'

She stirred, as, bending over her, Charles spoke. 'Aunt Julie. You have a visitor. His Majesty, King Louis-Philippe of France.'

Her eyes moved vacantly from one to the other. Her voice came low, hesitant, searching. 'Louis-Philippe? King of France? Louis-Philippe . . . Duc d'Orléans . . . ?'

As her nephew stepped aside, His Majesty took her hand. 'Yes, my beloved little friend, Louis-Philippe . . .'

A smile crossed her face. 'Sir . . . I . . . I am very proud.' Her voice suddenly seemed to gain strength. 'I regret, Sir . . . I am unable to make my curtsey . . .'

He pressed her hand. 'When you are well, dear Comtesse, and you are back at Court . . .'

She raised her eyes to meet his with a hint of amused disbelief . . . then they drooped in utter weariness.

She knew she would never make that curtsey.

On the following pages are details of some recent Arrow Romances from Hurst & Blackett

FOR THE BEST OF REASONS

by Jane Wallace

Anna's mother has died giving birth to her. As she grows up, although there is no material lack, she feels that her father resents her because of her resemblance to her mother.

In Florence, where she goes to study art, she meets Sean, a writer, and in her need for love she has an affair with him. The birth of their child brings a painful maturity to Anna but not to Sean, who is unable to face the responsibility.

How she attains fulfilment and happiness and overcomes the barrier between herself and her father makes a moving story.

The atmosphere of Florence is clearly drawn, and for light relief there is the delightful Mamma Stroumillo and her family with whom Anna lives for part of the time.

THE MAGNOLIA ROOM

by Annette Eyre

Beside the fountain in the Piazza della Signoria there is an inscription recording the fact that here, in 1498, Girolamo Savonarola was burned at the stake. It was a reminder to Kate Adamson that things had always been worse for someone.

The Magnolia Room is the poignant and dramatic story of a nice, ordinary, middle-class English girl who is blindly and hopelessly in love with an Italian noble-man. It is a case of love at first sight, but a love condemned by its unorthodox beginning. The Manzinis are one of the grandest families in Florence and their marriages are carefully arranged.

'How could I possibly be so unsuitable?' Kate cried in despair.

'You're up to your neck in something you don't begin to understand,' Charles, the English student working in the market, said.

There is Dino's friend, Giuseppe, the priest who ought to be on their side. Dino's aunt Mimma, who understands. Dino's little sister, made bewildered and unhappy. The old grandmother, craggy as a rock and as formidable. Dino's beautiful, determined mother. And Simona, the other woman.

Dino and Kate make a hero and heroine who tear at the reader's emotions. In a world that is hung up on class and privilege, religion and history, the young people only want each other. The outcome of the battle may come as a surprise to most readers who will feel Annette Eyre has written here her most touching and memorable book.

THE WILDERNESS WALK

by Sheila Bishop

A beautiful girl is seen sitting in the garden of an isolated cottage at the centre of a wood. Half an hour later she has vanished into thin air.

The disappearance of Ada Gainey has all the ingredients of a classic mystery. A fashionable courtesan, an ornament of Regency London, she has come down to the village of Cleave with her lover, Jack Eltham. When she disappears, he is distracted with grief. Lord Francis Aubrey, Jack's uncle and trustee, seems strangely unconcerned—but Lord Francis is an ambiguous character whose plausible theories will not stand up to the evidence of an unexpected witness, a young woman called Caroline Prior.

Caroline is visiting Devonshire with her married sister Lavinia, and Lavinia's four children, to enjoy the benefits of sea-bathing. It is not their first encounter with the Aubrey family, and partly for this reason Caroline soon finds herself directly involved in a drama of conflicting personalities and an extraordinary confusion of motives.

A TIME TO HEAL

by Clare Emsley

A time to heal . . . as a nurse in a fashionable London nursing home, or in Mydonia, the wild little country behind its mountain barrier? To Tessa, the doctor's daughter, it was a challenge—the known and the unknown. But Mydonia was not the only unknown quantity. For what of Mark Daventry, the eminent surgeon, for whom she would work in the hospital he had founded? Mark, brilliant and aloof, who had given up a career in Harley Street to devote himself to the warmhearted people to whom he was almost a god.

A time to heal . . . but for Mark, was that possible? Had the wound of his disastrous marriage to Francine gone too deep?

A time to heal . . . Francine herself, wayward and unpredictable, with an irresistible fascination for men.

A time to heal . . . when danger threatened Mydonia and Paul, the ruler's son, stood at the helm.

THE DOCTOR'S MARRIAGE

by Norah C. James

This is the story of a Group practice of doctors in London. Elizabeth, until recently a Sister in a large training hospital, has just married Michael Pelham, one of the partners, and now acts as secretary to the Group. She and Michael are deeply in love, but they discover a problem between them which, at one time, threatens their whole married existence. Then, in a mad moment, Elizabeth becomes involved with another man and her life becomes a nightmare until her problem is solved dramatically.

The novel moves against a background of doctors and patients, their lives and individual hopes, fears, joys and sorrows.

CACTUS ISLAND

by Barbara Kaye

Joanna arrives to start work for a Caribbean company, to find tropical life is not all glamour. Her reception is odd and disturbing, and not all the people she meets— even her own sister—are what they seem. Parties have undercurrents of gossip and scandal and a web of intrigue closes in on the romance which flowers quickly for her in the tropical sunshine. Under that same sun, turned merciless, she finds herself lost, panic-stricken and in possession of a dangerous secret, among the giant cacti or Coraiba—barbed symbols of an island which has worse terror in store.

But she no longer has to face it alone, and release comes for her and the others in the net, from the least expected quarter.

DOCTOR'S FOLLY

by Sonia Deane

Doctor Clive Wells and his wife, Fabia, are in practice together, but their work is their only point of contact, as their marriage deteriorates, reaching a crisis when Fabia suggests a revolutionary experiment in an attempt to avert divorce.

Far from saving their relationship, Fabia plunges it into greater jeopardy when Arden Melville comes into the picture and as Clive's patient, endangers not only his marriage, but his career, since Arden's husband, Giles, is determined to ruin Clive.

Doctor's Folly emphasises the tragedy of misunderstanding; the stupidity of believing that marriage can be manoeuvred to suit individual defects. Above all, that doctors, in particular, are immune from the temptations provided by their amorous patients.

This is one of Sonia Deane's most powerful novels which is bound to cause controversy and hold the reader's interest to the last page.